I0764646

THE VIRTUE TRANSITION

Novels by Dennis Bowen

International Thriller Series

THE WATER DIAMONDS
Book 1

THE BLACKSTONE PERFECTION
Book 2

THE CRYSTAL SEDUCTION
Book 3

THE REDROCK QUARANTINE
Book 4

THE FINAL MASQUERADE
Book 5

THE VIRTUE TRANSITION
Book 6

The Backstory Files

STONES
Book 1

THE VIRTUE TRANSITION

Dennis Bowen

The Virtue Transition is a work of fiction. Names, characters, places, and incidents are the products of the author's imagination or are used fictitiously. Any resemblance to actual events, locales, or persons, living or dead, is entirely coincidental.

ISBN: 978-1-7325610-0-7

FIRST EDITION

www.facebook.com/DennisBowenThrillers

www.twitter.com/DBowenThrillers

www.DennisBowen.com

Book Interior Design by 52 Novels

ACKNOWLEDGMENTS

Thank you to the readers who have immersed themselves in my *International Thriller Series.* While I create the intrigues that span the globe and enjoy every minute of it, in the end, I write these novels for you and your enjoyment, it's that simple.

As with *The Water Diamonds, The Blackstone Perfection, The Crystal Seduction, The Redrock Quarantine,* and *The Final Masquerade,* my appreciation and gratitude goes out to those who offered suggestions and encouragement during the writing of *The Virtue Transition.*

I express appreciation to my fabulous editor, Laura Taylor. She has provided the editing prowess to insure a quality presentation for this series and for STONES of *The Backstory Files.*

As in life, each successive endeavor—such as writing a series of novels—is built on what came before. Any errors or omissions in *The Virtue Transition* I claim as my own.

Once again, I extend my gratitude to family members and friends for their support, and to former colleagues, some of whom offered up their lives in the service of this great country, and whose presence in my life gives my International Thriller Series its noted sense of reality. Thank you to all.

—Dennis Bowen

CHAPTER 1

"I met someone."

The man seated across from the stoic woman said nothing. Like her, he stared down at the paint-chipped and splintered picnic table.

That three little words could cause so much damage was unknown to them. Previous to today, the highest impact three little words had been "I love you" spoken at their wedding.

Silence followed by more silence.

She stood and turned, exhaling, depleted.

She watched the nearby lake as its waves lapped at the water's edge, but heard nothing.

Even the birds in the eighty-foot pine tree not ten feet away waxed quiescent.

A distant buzz, probably teens playing with toy aircraft, penetrated the gloomy mood.

"It … it …"

"I want to hear," he whispered. "Tell me."

A gust blew past, tossing a loose paint chip to the ground. That covert team member, Lenny Lipschitz, had applied cheap paint over the original redwood as a gesture of friendship didn't matter.

To Hekka Crayle, the table symbolized their relationship. Once strong. Once steady. Now, coming apart. Unraveling.

"I need to know," said the man she'd grown to love. To fight alongside. To fight for.

"I can't, Magus … I … uh …"

The percussion of the next moment stopped the discussion dead.

It nearly stopped *them* dead.

One of five armed drones plowed into the tree, gusted there by the wind. There, to explode.

Crayle yanked Hekka's arm just in time. He rolled right.

Damaged, the tree shook, then emitted an explosive sound of its own.

Two seconds later, another loud crack. The tree leaned. The third crack was final.

The crashing pine missed the Crayles. Barely. It hit their log cabin dead on.

"*Micmac! Phoebe! They're inside!*"

They glanced back in the direction of the attack.

Two of the four armed drone escorts had splintered and fallen from the blast.

Switching to Plan B, the other two opened fire. Caliber .22 rounds arrayed inside their fuselages provided a barrage of deadly potential.

The Crayles fought to protect each other from the fusillade.

Inside the cabin, former SEAL/UDT veteran Micmac and current on-leave FBI Agent Phoebe had been working on a covert ops training video.

The explosion outside should have blown the sliding door and adjacent glass window into deathly shards. Bullet proof, bomb proof, they held strong. The roof, however, had not been strengthened to stop a huge falling tree six feet in girth.

The two dove away from each other. An instinctive ploy such that one or the other might survive.

Having landed in the kitchen, Phoebe forced open the side door and skirted the cabin.

Pinned by the couch that had slammed the wall, Micmac heard his ops game continue unabated with its own gunfire and explosions.

The last thing he heard before passing out—two booming shots. He smiled. His world went dark.

Phoebe had limped alongside the cabin to its rear. She took in the drones fixated on Crayle and Hekka. Micmac had heard Phoebe's .45 caliber Glock speak.

FBI colleagues referred to her as Annie Oakley for her deadly accuracy.

Two shots. Two drones.

Offshore, a camouflage-dressed man fired up his boat's three Mercury outboards and sped off.

A similarly clad cohort flew a sixth drone, its video streaming into her Smartphone complete, into the waves. The diminutive woman smiled, threw her drone controller into the lake, and ducked out of sight.

Crayle would never forget the flag hanging from the craft's stern.

He rolled his head to the right. To where his pregnant wife had landed.

Gone.

Having slammed his head against the picnic bench, he fought for consciousness.

A light snow began, the season's first.

He begged a desperate pair of eyes for clarity instead of the fog.

No Hekka.

"Where …" he gasped. "… where …"

The usual was no longer that. Normal would be anything but. Peace of mind. Tranquility. Relegated to hopes and dreams once more. After all. They were Magus and Hekka Crayle.

CHAPTER 2

"Jack's going to kill me," Crayle moaned under the weight of the crushed picnic table. He referenced the owner of the property, which included his own just-devastated residence, a separate garage about fifty feet distant, and fifty feet from that, the Big House. Jack Sommers stayed in the latter when not hard at work in the Washington, D.C. environs.

His mind worked its way around the situation as he shoved aside the table remnants. The simple physical effort caused his mind to shift into reverse.

"I'm going to kill Jack for this." Crayle seemed to be setting a mental date certain. A voice interrupted his train of thought.

Hekka, having heard booms from a Glock, headed to Phoebe's side of the cabin. Not for herself, but to protect her baby. Their baby. There, the two pregnant women hunkered down.

Crayle heard her cry, "Magus!"

He took the long way around the tree and found them. Hekka and Phoebe, both nearing the end of their pregnancies, attempting a 'thank goodness we're safe' hug.

"You're both okay?"

His wife looked up at him. "Yes, but …"

He sensed her anxiety. She was afraid to look.

She glanced down. Hekka touched her abdomen. "Please tell me you're alive!"

"They've gone. Other than a severe headache, I'm okay."

Phoebe spoke. "We'll keep our eyes out."

Rather than add to the scrum, Crayle ducked in through the blown out side door. The tree had knocked out power, but light wasn't a problem. The caved-in roof didn't keep much of it out.

Crayle knelt beside Micmac, oblivious to the intermittent snowfall.

The former sailor roused, and pushed a tree branch away from his face. "Is that dandruff on your head, or is it really snowing?"

"Early Fall. Any flakes I have will last longer than this dusting of snow. You bleeding anywhere? Anything broken?"

"No. The couch cushioned the blow. Kind of untidied your cabin, though."

The once wall-adorning collector plates decorated the living room. In shards. They'd already been shot to pieces with automatic weapons during a previous attack. Micmac had made the necessary reconstruction such that they'd appeared virgin new. Until now.

"Is it safe to come in?" asked Phoebe.

"Yeah. You'll have to step over the tree."

The women entered what remained of the kitchen.

"How about a couple of beers?" Micmac hollered. "While you're in there."

Crayle chuckled. "What the hell did I start? Did any of you see that boat? With the flag? We don't get foreign flags on boats in Big Bear. Stars on a blue background, and a Union Jack in the corner."

Micmac, a master of esoterica, answered. "Aussie, my friend. Australian."

Crayle's mind turned to another subject. "You were saying? You met someone?" he said in a matter of fact tone.

"I received a call this morning, while you slept, Magus. I … it was a special ring tone. He … he was never to use it … unless … "

"Who was it? And what did he say?"

"Here." She passed a folded note. "I can't even repeat it. I wrote it down."

He reached for the piece of paper, scanning her countenance as he did.

This had to be bad. The fingers of a man who'd been through every stage of hell on multiple occasions trembled for the first time. His mind felt numb, but ready to perceive. His heart wanted none of it.

He entered what was left of the kitchen and staggered back, holding a towel against a bloodied head. "Hope Jack has insurance for a tree house."

Laughter broke through.

Crayle shook his head. "Two men with headaches and head damage, and two women pregnant. I'm sure Lenny could make something out of that."

"Jeez-Louise!" Lenny entered through the rubble. "I know you wanted that tree gone, but you shouldn't have opted for one of those 'don't try this at home' solutions. All together. Don't … try … this … at … home."

They would have done him in. Right there. If they could.

CHAPTER 3

Later that day, Magus Crayle and Lenny Lipschitz sat on the ground, their backs against a still-standing cabin wall. Crayle put the obvious question in play.

"Who could have done this?"

"We've been up against bad players all over the world, but what about someone new. What about the Russians?"

"What's the possibility that the Russian president is Illuminé?"

"Not possible," Lenny responded. "He'd have to be an atheist, and a thug."

"The Communists who ruled for seventy years had to have absolute authority. The Orthodox church promulgated morality. Not just any morality. That from a higher source than humanity. The supreme source."

"What did that mean, exactly?"

"It meant that Orthodoxy morals trumped Communist morals, or lack of them. The communists became Atheists R Us as far as Russia was concerned."

"Not necessarily a thug, though."

"Former KGB."

"Oh."

"Forget him for now," Crayle admonished. "I called the Quarry hospital. They're sending an ambulance for us. Please, Lenny, pick up all the drone parts. Tell the authorities, who are no doubt dealing with the brush fire in the hills southeast of Sugarloaf and slow to respond, the tree was struck by lightning. That's why it caved. They'll ask about injuries. This is important. No one was hurt. Got it?"

The ambulance slid into the driveway. The crew of two gathered the Crayles and the MacKays, just making it onto the road and around a corner when a sheriff's unit pulled in. The two officers took a jaw-dropped view of the damage.

"I realize you can't remove a tree to get an unobstructed lake view, but this seems a bit drastic. Where are the owners?"

Lenny checked his watch. "They're out of town. Oh, and no one's hurt."

Technically, they were out of town. Just.

CHAPTER 4

The boat that returned to the popular and busy Holloway's Marina no longer sported the flag of a foreign country. It had been swapped for its American counterpart. No one noticed the man and woman tying up, and stepping off.

"Mission accomplished?" asked the man with a refined, yet strong, accent. His associate, young enough to be his daughter, found it at times difficult to understand.

"Quick. We must hustle across Big Bear Lake before the local constabulary can be notified and respond. The normal collapse of a giant pine can explain the horrendous crash they must have heard the two-point-five miles across the lake and the seven miles to the east end."

"You, my dear, are a genius. A deadly genius. It must have been difficult not to include death in the plan. It is cold in this place. My Smartphone indicates forty-five degrees Fahrenheit. I can't wait to get home to the incessant warmth."

"I chose the late Fall time of year to minimize the number of boats in proximity to our assault. Since everyone has a cell phone these days, any eye witness could describe us and our use of drones for the attack while also providing viable images. They could notify the sheriff long before we would be able to make port on the south side."

"We'll be fine. No one saw us. Except our targets."

"No matter. We're leaving. Too bad we can't stick around to see what they do next."

"Rather risky. You could've killed them."

"You know how good I am. All risks calculated and allowed for."

"You hit the tree on purpose, didn't you?"

"I expected the boom, but an eighty foot tree shouldn't crash down from the small amount of C-4 I used. Anyways, my final drone set down its camera in the bushes before I deep sixed it. Here, check this out." She withdrew her Smartphone.

"Except for the snow, I can see the back of the cabin. There! That's Mr. Crayle. He's saying something. Calling out. Can you get the audio?"

"Seriously?" She packed away her phone. "Let's go find a quiet place."

He knew what that meant. And after, perhaps a trip down from the mountain resort to the Outback Restaurant he'd researched on Yelp. "In a place called San Bernardino. Hospitality Lane."

CHAPTER 5

Lenny and Alona attempted to resume a semblance of tranquility at their Big Bear cabin on the south side of the lake. Things had quieted down at the Crayle residence to their north. The sheriff and his posse returned to business as usual after a string of calls and a conversation with the President of the United States.

Alona watched as Lenny sauntered into the kitchen, ostensibly to check progress on lunch.

"It is time … for me to whine," he rapped.

Alona paused.

"Boomp. Boomp. Boomp."

She spun, hands waving.

"No, no, no, no, no! No, no! There will be absolutely no rap-whining in this household!"

He twirled. "Boomp. Boomp."

"Nothing of the sort." She placed her paring knife back in the block, then brandished her new selection, a butcher knife. "*Nichts, keine, nichevo.*" She paused, pressing her pursed lips to one side, as if to access other language synonyms. She glanced at a wine bottle on the counter. "*Far niente!*" She particularly liked the Italian, and waved her free hand in the air. "*Far niente!*"

"All that work and all you can come up with is a lot of nothing." He laughed at his own joke.

"Micmac loves research. I asked him for admonishments in foreign languages. Gave 'im a list."

"Oh? Admonish this ..."

"Let me see that finger again," she said as she approached, waving the knife.

"Drone," Lenny interrupted.

"You're saying that I tend to drone on?"

"No! I'm hearing a drone!"

Alona sniffed. "Did you just fart?"

"It was the dog."

"We don't have a dog."

"I was thinking of getting one."

Lenny glanced over to see if his misdirection worked. It had.

"Yeah? What kind?"

"Bulldog. They fart. Provide cover."

"Swell."

Rescued from being impaled on a butcher knife by a special ring on his Smartphone, Lenny excused himself and stepped out onto his cabin's expansive wooden deck. Boulder Bay provided abundant natural and man-made beauty. As the home for fabricated log homes and for boats at nearby Holloway's Marina, it sat in quiet comfort on the southwest aspect of Big Bear Lake.

Every once in a while, Alona would glance out the window. Characteristically, Lenny became more and more animated. It came easy for him to explain in detail why the counterparty to a conversation was wrong, and he was right. So far, he'd received no death threats, but there was still time on his clock.

After fifteen minutes, he stepped back inside. Uncharacteristically, he didn't speak a word.

"Okay. Okay. What was that one about?" Alona finally asked.

He just sat on the couch, saying nothing.

"I said ..."

He blinked. "Oh, did you say something?"

"Yes. Something like, would you please hand me my other butcher knife? It's not nearly as sharp."

"All right. It was just ... just ... an old case. Back East. Looks like I'm going to have to go back there for a few days."

"You don't have any more cases. The Lipschitz investigative enterprise is no more." She paused. "It is, isn't it?"

"Sure. We folded it up. You did the legal. No, it's just one of my dad's old clients. Needs a bit of help. I worked on the case, so I have specific knowledge, but it's sensitive. Can't put it in an email, or discuss over the phone. You can get along without me for a couple of days, can't you?"

"No sex for a couple of days? Hmmm. How about I just lop off your so-called valuables to keep myself entertained. That was rhetorical."

"By your leave, Your Excellency, I'm going to go pack some duds. And you should like that I'll be saving us some money. I'll drive down the back way, Highway 18, to Jack's International air strip, and fly that gorgeous Falcon 8X."

"Flori can fix you cocktails while she's not in the flight deck piloting. Just keep your eyes off that Brazilian cleavage ..." She waved the butcher knife. "... or I'll be doing some cleaving of my own."

"I do love it when you talk sex."

He stood, and headed for the bedroom. He'd miss her, but this was not optional. If she were to learn what really was transpiring, there'd be hell to pay. And cleaving.

CHAPTER 6

The royal palace in Stockholm emanated a quiet splendor. It opened for business in 1754, but updates over the centuries brought it up to par with the newer edifices of Sweden's grand city. The passage of Autumn ensured that all of the fireplaces would be stocked full of logs set aflame, had so-called environmentalists not rallied for their replacement with gas inserts.

Quite traditional, the queen fully intended to rectify that situation the following Spring. She, with assistance from her closest ally, one Jean-Marc Lalumière, planned to rehire the royal woodsmen to stock the reserves.

Jean-Marc fully believed that his father, Sylvain, and step-mother Pattie Norbrunn, inseparable, were killed in the Monaco explosion a few months earlier. Pope and Prince, too. Now, he resided with the Swedish Queen, but needed to schedule a coronation. His own. To do that, he would need to co-opt the new pope, Alighieri, to bless the ceremony and crown him as King of France.

Such were the thoughts occupying a quite tall, youngish man with aspirations. To experience them in a sumptuous royal bedroom with a real queen seemed appropriate. He felt anxious, yet confident. Ready.

He tossed back the bedcovers and exited the royal bed. Arriving at a stone wall thirty feet away, he unlatched the leaded glass window and swung it open.

"It's turning, the weather."

The few snowflakes that blew in on him didn't seem to have much effect.

"How did you know I was awake?"

"You stopped repeating, 'Oh, Jean-Marc!' over and over."

"Hmm. I'm still the queen. Hand me that scepter from the wall adornment, so I may crown you."

"Crowning is in my blood, it seems. Not long ago, I sat with my father and his true love, my former mistress."

"Why is that special? Did you impregnate the woman?"

"We sat at a very special table on a purpose-built platform perched just above the catacombs of Rome's Colosseum. I thought I told you this story."

"Purpose-built? To what purpose?"

"With two very special guests."

"Was it this Magus Crayle you obsess over all the time?"

"He was there, as was his quite lovely wife, Hekka. I believe her name comes from the Finnish."

The Swedish queen bristled.

"In any event, they were held quite secure—unable to move. But the two to whom I referred were the Pope and the Prince of Monaco. Like yourself, he was part of the dwindling remainder of European monarchs. In short, the two of them performed the marriage of my father and Ms. Norbrunn, declaring them King and Queen of France."

"I remember now. I have heard this before."

He turned his naked body toward her.

"I've also related how the old and exiled democratic leadership of France travelled to China, apparently to convince my countrymen that they remained relevant and still in charge."

"And as reports have confirmed, the entirety of the French government hierarchy perished in the nuclear detonation over Xian. It also took the lives of the new Emperor of China, Chin Yao-wu. And his general, Li."

"Yes, my love. That momentous occasion, plus the latest bomb in Monte Carlo, sets you and I up in what the Americans call the catbird seat."

"Catbird? My American doesn't get much past hot dogs."

"The new king and queen, from all I can tell, died in Monaco. Turned to vapor, as they say."

"I see. So we prove first that they were legitimately crowned monarch heads of state for France. Barring any other contenders that might pop up, you are the rightful heir to the throne. I truly get the madness."

"My father was proclaimed king by the Prince of Monaco. The ultra-ordained and infallible pope seconded the motion. They married the two. I have it all on video."

He fetched his Smartphone from a nightstand and played the entire scene. The elation showed on his face.

"What about the bodies?"

He blanched. "Bodies? Why, vaporized means no bodies. But the Formula One photographers and those in attendance from the media streamed the action right up to the flash of light."

"You realize, we can't afford any mistakes. Not one."

"Yes. But if we get this right, I will have France!"

"And I already have Sweden!"

They looked deeply into each other's eyes.

They clasped hands, chorusing, "Then, we marry!"

CHAPTER 7

Time to leave Saint Petersburg and head back to Moscow. Vladimir, President of the Russian Federation, had one last chore. He needed to meet with the czarina. A great deal was at stake. He could transition from a current and prospective moderate legacy to one of world class.

He recalled his conversation not long before with his number one advisor. Raspi would not be allowed to attend the meet. Nor would anyone else. What would be discussed would be the Top Secret of Top Secrets.

The trip from Saint Petersburg to the venerable Catherine's Palace provided just enough time for Vladimir to compose his thoughts. What would transpire on this day would determine his future. And hers.

He'd not experienced monarchy either in its splendor nor its decadence. To be revered rather than to be elected appealed to his ego. A carriage of gold versus a hardened limousine. An imperial guard instead of body guards.

When his small caravan pulled to within visual distance, he felt further overwhelmed. The palace itself seemed to reach out, to tempt him as would a mistress. He knew from his FSB intelligence head that the building extended a full 1,056.25 feet. Whether in feet or the 325 meter equivalent, it beat hands down the upscale suburban dacha he'd occupied during his Soviet days. The powder blue exterior with substantive white trim intimated at perfection within. Soft regal, he labeled it.

In that instant, he recognized it. The essence of it all. Class. Royals possessed innate class. Something the leaders of his country had never possessed. Not even in trace amounts.

It all tied in. Reflecting back to post-revolution times, the ruling class had been rejected most violently for the working class. Although necessary, the workers lacked class. Not their thing, as the Americans would say.

But when he watched the English royalty, he felt envy. The workers revered and cherished them. No one would overthrow them. So, what had Russia accomplished? Vladimir had done as well as one could under the communist umbrella, and since. Still, to what end?

The end game came into sharp focus. He stood to gain both class and the reverence of his people if only his grand scheme bore fruit.

When his motorcade drew to a sudden halt, Vlad knew he'd drifted into a daydream. Fine. Had not the West pointed out since its creation that life was all about one's dreams? Perhaps the greatest unmentioned flaw in his old ideology was the death of the dream. Give what you can, they'd said. Take only what you need, they'd said. To Hell with a better tomorrow. In fact, to hell with Hell. They'd even killed off religious morality and replaced it with the Marxist code.

Vlad's body convulsed him awake. The czarina stood before him, leaning down.

"Good. You've regained consciousness. Clear the cobwebs, as they say, and we can begin our deliberations. Perhaps even design the future."

Vlad realized he'd fallen asleep. It was not unusual at all. His premier aide, Raspi, would … where was he? Vlad's head whipped around, searching for the one man who, among other duties, served as his anchor.

"Your man is downstairs at ground level," came the czarina's soft voice.

Vlad surveyed the room once more.

"And so is your protective unit. You were carried up the stairway and down the hall, past all of my imperial guardsmen, to this my meeting room. You are quite safe."

Reality struck him like an Oklahoma tornado. If she'd wanted him dead, the heavy breathing he now experienced would have been superfluous. Curtailed. Counting his good fortune thus far, he began the conversation.

"If I may address you as Your Highness, I must be off shortly to Moscow. My duties there beckon."

She'd moved behind him, perhaps to pour them a calming drink. He'd seen the decanter earlier while searching the room for answers.

"Continue. Please," came from behind.

"I will be succinct. If you must have further details, please interrupt."

He heard a brief laugh.

"When one is the monarch, he or she never interrupts."

"Ah. Because you want to hear all that is said."

"Because the monarch, by definition, is incapable of interrupting. It is as if God has spoken when she utters even a single syllable. If He interrupted one of your pronouncements, you would not refer to it as an interruption. Inspiration. Commandment. Anything but an interruption."

"Should we agree here on a mutual course of action, I may ask you for your valuable insights as to how monarchs behave."

"And by your inference, you have come to discuss the potential for myself as monarch of all Russia, and the integral part you wish to play should that result come to pass."

She stepped in front of him. She held a Catherine's Palace shot glass in each hand, and passed one to him.

They tinked, then quaffed.

He stared.

She stood before him stark naked. "Like Catherine before me, I prefer to bond in bed."

He still struggled to regain control of his lower jaw.

"Make love to me, Vladimir. Then, let's you and I make love to Mother Russia."

And it came to pass. They made love and, in loving whispers, formulated the successor to the Russian Federation.

More than satisfied with the outcome, he channeled long ago emperor, Julius Caesar. "I came, I saw, I conquered."

The czarina interrupted his smile.

"Not quite. You saw. You came. The conquest? Our conquest? We shall see."

She glanced around the pale blue room with its ornate, arctic white adornments. And with the gold embellishments tastefully applied throughout. Was there a suitable palace in Moscow. Or would she simply move the capitol to Saint Petersburg?

Vladimir had no such worries. His sense of humor broke through. "What we just did in this bed was exceptional. It was great. But …" He turned to her with his own slightly wicked smile. "I don't even know your name."

He chuckled.

She followed suit.

Then, a sobering thought. When the time came, would she have him killed … or do it herself?

CHAPTER 8

The miniature nuclear bomb that exploded beneath Beijing transformed a quasi-communist/capitalist authoritarian regime into a vacant empire with its major governing elite, the Standing Committee, displaced and the bulk of the ruling party destroyed. Chin Yao-wu had utilized the Blackstone Strategy of CIA magician Magus Crayle to its fullest. Few knew that Chin made serious international enemies in the process.

The consequence of making the wrong enemies, however, destroyed Chin and the entire leadership of France in a second bomb dropped from a restored German Stuka dive bomber on the ancient capitol, Xian. The devastating blow elevated Chin's young wife, Ling An-yee, to the position of empress. Instead of liquidating the captured Standing Committee remnants, she chose to utilize them as a Chief Executive Officer would utilize a Chief Operating Officer in a corporation. They possessed the requisite experience with the people. Of managing them. Of containing them. Their proven abilities prompted her necessary and straight-forward choice.

The new day brought sunshine to Hong Kong island, the current site of China's governance. The typical fog that hovered over the city below Victoria Peak and its palace slowly began to burn off. Viewing the process each time was as if the first. It was the great reveal of one of the world's premier cities. It also represented the great reveal to the governed below of the palace of their empress.

"With both Beijing and Xian gone, I'm having to operate from Hong Kong. At least, while a new palace is created for me. I'm thinking some place different, like in the province Hebei ... or in Shanghai."

Empress Ling stood before her palace window, gazing across Hong Kong's Victoria Harbour to Kowloon and the New Territories. As was typical, she spoke her thoughts to an empty room.

"I continue to bring adopted girls, at age 13, and add them to the colorful rainbow of twelve as did my late husband. As with him, no sexual anything for them. Just a great education and loyal service thereafter. Each will become adept in a martial art suited precisely to that individual. Still, I struggle with the notion of training the Death Touch, as I learned. It is too easy for one to disable me, and then kill."

Startled by the presence of someone entering the huge room, she whipped around, ready to admonish. The cheongsam dress worn by the entrant was enhanced with gold embellishments, a sign that the wearer was at least eighteen years old. The color denoted serious significance.

"Oh. Please make noise or ask permission to enter, White Daughter. My nerves are still in disarray after receiving the news."

"I am so sorry. Chin was like a father to us. Our adoption made it legal, but he saw that we had everything. The education, the ..."

"Yes, he was a good man. So generous."

"And when the bombs of the man you knew, Mr. Crayle, pushed aside the Communists, he elevated father Chin Yao-wu to Emperor Chin. No one could have predicted that outcome."

"The man you mentioned predicted it. It was the manifestation of the Crayle Blackstone Strategy."

White Daughter nodded affirmation, but added, "I abstained from the politics and schemes. Was I wrong to do so?"

"You were destined to be his concubine by the imperial color of your garment. White. Number One. To conceive his firstborn."

"That is why I have come today."

Ling wrinkled her brow. "You slept with him but once. Surely …"

White's head sank to her chest.

"There's no way."

Ling stood astounded for a few seconds. She'd just become Empress as dictated by Chin's dramatic demise in Xian. Now, a game-changer. Big time.

She moved to White Daughter, putting her arm around her.

"Here. Come sit down."

She guided the eighteen-year-old to a sixteenth century sofa. Then, walked around behind.

"Lean back." She took a handful of White's long, glistening hair, careful not to pull and alert her.

With her right hand, she pressed around the narrow neck, and pushed her fingers into the space between the tendon and esophagus.

"There, there. This will relax you. Remove your deep tensions regarding your … our dilemma."

White processed the seeming enigmatic statement.

Ling brought pressure on the carotid artery.

The younger woman reached up. She clasped Ling's hand. To no avail.

Chin had seen to his adopted daughters' education in both knowledge base, and a martial art chosen specifically for each girl.

White's had been the graceful White Crane style of Kung Fu developed by female martial artist, Fang Qiniang. Evade, then attack opponents vulnerabilities. Not useful in this configuration.

Ling, in those earlier days known as Black Daughter, learned the infamous *Dim Mak*. The Death Touch.

To take someone to unconsciousness, one released one's arterial pressure as soon as the target passed out due to the deprived blood supply to the brain.

Ling did not release. If she did, White's child would become the new emperor.

She increased the pressure. Prolonging would cause brain damage at first, then death. The fetus would follow. No one would know. The perfect solution.

"No!" Ling cried out. "*No!*"

Quickly, she released her grip, and began to slap her fingers against the carotid-jugular-vagus nerve bundle. To stimulate. To increase blood flow.

"Oh." White lifted her head as consciousness returned.

Ling walked around the sofa, took White's shoulders, and laid her down.

"You had a faint, but you'll feel better now. There. Retire to your room. Rest. For both of you."

• • •

Later in a specially-constructed sound and technology isolated room, the empress engaged in her constitutional tête-à-tête with her most trusted confidant.

"White Daughter carries the former emperor's baby," Ling posed to Yellow. "So, shall I become the Dowager Empress by the time I reach 21, relegated to waiting until the baby boy is born?"

Yellow drew a deep breath, then shrugged. "I am surely not qualified to speculate for that which you contemplate."

"Yellow, I must talk to Magus, I mean, Mr. Crayle. You remember him, don't you? During the two year period that he provided strategy and tactics to Emperor Chin, he mentored me."

Yellow Daughter did not react to the implication of former intimacy between the two. She knew. She remembered a lot more than might be healthful. She was sure Mr. Crayle had been, indeed, quite the mentor to the young woman, then known to all as Black Daughter. Now, Empress Ling An-yee needed him. Yellow would see that this did not bring insoluble problems. First, she needed to obey.

The gold Smartphone encrusted with all manner of precious gems did sport a heft. Ling touched the requisite stones in the proper order. It not only emitted her speed-dialed request into the ether, but assured that all traffic in their conversation would be double encrypted.

The device's response a few seconds later, "Line is busy." Crayle's voice. She recognized it immediately. She'd expected to hear him speak for real. And to perform the Claptonesque handshake they'd arranged:

"It's late in the evening," she would say.

"She's wond'ring what clothes to wear," he'd reply.

Had she been given to vulgar outbursts, now would have been the perfect time.

She glanced to Yellow. "That will be all, for now. I'll hang on to the phone for when he calls back."

Yellow Daughter bowed, then backed herself out of the room via a Ming Period set of very expensive drapes.

Now, comfortable that she was the sole occupant of the room, Ling, Empress of all China, whispered, "Call me, Magus."

CHAPTER 9

A fresh new Autumn day dawned on the Big Bear Valley. Sunshine and scattered clouds, the forecast for the day, did not disappoint.

As Crayle walked the circumference of his cabin, it became clear that some major lifting would be required to restore it to livable.

He strode across Jack Sommers' lakeside compound and past the standalone garage. In keeping in construction components and style with the two living quarters, it sported horizontal log sides with a pent roof. What a visual glance didn't reveal was the two tunnels beneath that led in either direction to the large and the small cabins.

Care needed to be taken in the repairs to his cabin since the fallen pine tree had probably damaged the covert access to the tunnel. It seemed perfectly clear. He'd have to restrict the repair work to someone, or ones, he could trust implicitly. Micmac, the gadget man and former SEAL/UDT weapons specialist, topped the list.

As he reached the larger cabin with its prominent prow windows facing the lake, he knew who he needed to reel back in. To assist Micmac and himself on the rebuild.

He snatched the CIA Smartphone from his deep cargo shorts pocket, and touched in the speed dial numbers.

"Hi, Lenny. Hey, where did you go? Alona says she doesn't even know. Sabbatical?"

"Uh, I just needed to get away to finish some work. Uh, one of my dad's old clients."

"Well, where are you, and what's with all the 'Uh' stuff?" Crayle regretted reverting to the old spy tradecraft tactic of asking even team members questions to which you know the answer.

"Uh, back east."

"Playing hard to get, are we? What are you doing in Savannah, Georgia?"

"Uh …"

"C'mon, Lenny. Give."

"Okay. Okay. The short story is that I'm skip-tracing Heidi."

"My voice stress analysis app indicates that her name isn't Heidi."

"She uses that name and works out of Switzerland."

"So, that's not her real name, and she isn't Swiss."

"Don't you just love this spy shit?"

"Your father's company was Silberweiss and Son Private Investigations, if I recall. Not real spying."

"Trust me."

"I believe your wife misses you."

"Alona would join me on this one, if it weren't for her condition."

"Pregnant women, at least as far as nine months, can actually function. Hekka and Phoebe haven't skipped a beat."

"Well, she's got a client on top of that."

"Oh."

"Uh, gotta go, Mag, but keep me up to speed if Jack comes up with anything new."

"Will do, Lenny. Stay safe."

"Uh, yeah. You, too."

Lenny clicked off. He glanced across the dock as the Georgia Queen tri-level paddle wheeler tied up. As the stevedores doubled up on the lines and connected to shore power, he realized it would be a long wait.

He'd just been a lot less than forthcoming with Magus Crayle, the triple-threat CIA operative that no one would want to run afoul of. And perhaps his best friend.

If only he hadn't been so trusting of the one who called herself Heidi. And her sister. A Swiss banker along with an information technology specialist. If only.

Investigations can only go so far. He could sure use his wife's sharp legal mind. Alona would dump her case load into Big Bear Lake, if he asked. He was sure of that. Whatever hardship she'd encounter on a flight back east, she'd endure. He was sure of that, too.

He lifted his phone to dial her. Before he could, it rang. **Heidi** popped up on his screen.

The call lasted all of two-and-a-half minutes. Most of it taken by Heidi interrupting Lenny's numerous questions with the German equivalent of Close Your Mouth.

When she rang off, he knew what he'd heard. Things were just a bit different than he'd originally been told. They would both have to be very careful—other eyes watched. He must follow every instruction in every detail, or the deal was off. Did he understand? She repeated that several times, perhaps for emphasis.

Fortunately, he'd experienced quasi-enigmatic situations before. First, as a private investigator in his father's firm, then as a member of the Crayle team. He could sum up what he'd just heard. This operation, as the team would characterize it, would not be nearly as easy as he'd imagined, or been led to believe.

CHAPTER 10

Lenny had crossed the gangway and stepped aboard the tourist river boat as directed by the call. He could swear that, as the lines were loosened and tossed aboard by the stevedores, he saw a just-debarked Heidi departing the dock area. He'd seen her just once before in Amsterdam.

The tall, slender blonde held something to her ear.

"The call!" blurted through Lenny's lips

The phone in his hand had continued to vibrate as he'd fallen into a state of mind Crayle deemed *brain fade*.

Once again, he answered in code. "This is LL1."

"HL1, here," she responded.

"That's you, isn't it?"

"I had to be sure you weren't followed."

"But this cruise will probably take two hours. And you're there. And I'm here. Where will we meet?"

"I've a place on Hilton Head."

"South Carolina?"

"Yes, that Hilton Head."

"But—"

He saw that she'd been joined by a brunette, shorter by two inches. Trouble?

He fetched his spy binoculars from his pocket and took a closer look. Oh, the younger woman wore a label on her windbreaker. UBER. He shook his head. A Swiss banker using ride share. Oh, well.

"Find your way to Harbour Town on the northwest aspect of the island. Then, the Quarterdeck Restaurant. Ask for reservations under *Loy.*" She realized she'd given the Swiss pronunciation. "Spelled L-E-U."

He knew her country boasted four cultures—German, French, Italian, and Romansh—he still couldn't place her accent. Perhaps from the western French zone of Switzerland. Montreux. Geneva. But then, the Germanic name, Heidi, made no sense. Perhaps named after an aunt from the Swiss northeast. No matter.

Legal help mattered, since the transaction would occur on American soil. Serious and discreet legal help.

He called Alona.

• • •

Back inside his rental, a metallic rust colored rental Buick Enclave, he observed the stately period architecture, for which Savannah was renowned, as he drove west. "Easy to see why folks want to live here," he said to the only one in the car.

The drive out of town onto Interstate 17 and north across the Savannah River posed no difficulties. Thank you, GPS, he thought to himself.

Thirty minutes later, he'd crossed to the South Carolina coast and out to the famous Hilton Head island. Certainly, the playground of the rich. Lots and lots of money here.

• • •

Finding his way to the designated meeting place proved not at all difficult. He drove onto Hilton Head island, paid the Sea Pines Plantation six dollar toll, tossed the black on yellow SEA PINES pass on the dash, and headed northwest. Ten minutes later, he spotted the lighthouse landmark in the distance with its red and white horizontal stripes, then found a parking spot at the Harbour Town marina. He'd discovered by way of his Smartphone on the way over, that the marina and this harbor had been designed around an old oak tree by plantation founder, Charles Fraser. So someone had saved a tree. He wondered if anyone would save him.

Lenny took a moment. On the heels of an excessively stressful and difficult day, he needed a break and saw just the ticket.

He smiled a bit. Under the circumstances as he knew them, he rested assured that the entire Crayle team would have chorused, "No!" They'd just have to learn to trust him, he thought.

Lenny's sunset cruise aboard The Spirit of Harbour Town was restful, or would have been, absent the enormity of the mission at hand. Reality struck. He wondered, how could he have screwed up so badly?

The GPS gods got him to the restaurant in short order, where he proceeded with Heidi's instructions.

As he approached the target—The Quarterdeck Waterfront Dining—he saw no signs of Heidi. Nor signs of any trouble. The marina and harbor appeared quiescent and beautiful. He imagined sitting in the restaurant someday with Alona, watching a stunning sunset. He fantasized owning a place on Sea Pines Plantation, and owning one of the radically expensive boats arrayed before him, which silently screamed, MONEY! But, business first.

Inside the Quarterdeck, a young man whose nameplate said Jack escorted Lenny to a table. The accent might be South African, he considered. For a second, the P.I. wondered about the other Jack. Did Jack Sommers, who now acted as head of the CIA, have children? Neither he nor his ex-wife, Marli, had said a thing on the subject. He decided to ask at the next opportunity.

Lenny settled into his chair in the not-quite-full and moderately vibrant restaurant, and his phone rang.

Heidi.

"Don't say a word. Place an order for Southern Fried Chicken for two. Then, one order each of She-Crab Bisque, Southern Fried Green Tomatoes, and Firecracker Gator Bites. Do not order the oysters on the half shell—you and I are not going there."

Click.

He glanced around at the upset neighbors due to his phone's obnoxious ring tone.

"Sorry."

He held it aloft as he pecked with his free hand.

"There. Vibrate."

He showed it to the circle of irate diners.

After placing the phone on vibrate, it did just that.

CHAPTER 11

Two of the Central Intelligence Agency's best, Magus Crayle and Jack Sommers, sat in their respective habitats, each holding a secure Smartphone to his ear.

With his own cabin uninhabitable, Crayle provided the acting director of the CIA with enough detail to warrant a sympathetic response. "Use my cabin until yours is back in service. You can supervise whatever needs to be supervised, and Hekka will be quite comfortable."

"I don't want to impose, but I know from what transpired back there at Langley, it might be a while before you can get back to Big Bear."

"Yeah. Go ahead. You know the secret way in. If the old code doesn't work, get onto my Company account in secure mode and look under the directory, Flower Pot. That'll get you done."

"Jack, we love the cabin here on the lake, but it's really yours. Hekka and I have made our temporary home at her ranch. Maybe Marli would like to move in."

"Great idea, Magus. She and my current wife, Flori, can share war stories."

"Hear me out. She has a place, due to her post CIA operative success as a real estate agent, on the beach in Malibu."

"So?"

"Realtors need an escape from time to time. A second place in the mountains, lakeside, would be perfect for her."

"I see. Then, she gets a boyfriend, and makes enough noise in the middle of the night to hear all the way across the compound through two sets of double-pane, bulletproof glass."

"She wouldn't do that."

"Wanna bet? I made a peace offering a couple of years ago. Sole access to an overseas account—don't ask, it's classified."

"For all the suffering she believes you caused, perhaps twenty bucks wasn't enough."

"Ha fucking ha. It was millions. Swiss Francs."

"A good currency, at the time."

"When I told her, she went to work on her phone. The calculator app." He affected a female voice. 'When I subtract out the interest I would've earned had I received this amount in a timely fashion, and divide by the years of pain … not enough.' Can you believe it?"

"I'll take the Fifth on that particular question. Let it sink in. Give it time. Consideration, okay?" Crayle felt himself reaching across the ether and touching Jack's arm.

"Yeah, all right. Oh, I almost forgot …"

"Yes. I know. The president needs my services yesterday. Let's talk later. I've got some work to do."

"I'll give your regards. Ciao."

Jack rang off.

Crayle took his advice and set up shop in the larger of the two lakeside cabins. The prow-shaped windows seem to rise fourteen or so feet, letting in plenty of precious light. The large deck replete with picnic table and benches, plus a state-of-the-art stainless steel grill, left little more to be desired. And that little more was covered by a back-opening refrigerator-freezer in the kitchen accessible from the deck.

Time for some peace and quiet. A treat in Crayle's life, he would not waste any opportunity to enjoy.

CHAPTER 12

Crayle pilfered the refrigerator for a cold bottle of Blue Moon Belgian White. On the sofa and ten minutes into a rerun of Gene Simmons' Private Parts, he heard a double knock. Then, Phoebe entered the magic security code and let herself in. Following the sounds of the television, she padded into the family room, took a quick look out at the lake, and sat carefully into an easy chair.

"Howdy, Mag. Where's the wife?"

"I believe she's out buying baby clothes."

"And didn't ask me. You can do better than that."

"I didn't say which baby she was buying them for."

"Another fabulous save, home boy. You should be saving all that resourcefulness for our next op."

"Think you could pass an operational readiness test with that future FBI Director getting ready to pop?"

"You're right. I need to take things down a notch or two. Sometime next year, though, I'll be raring to go. As long as world peace doesn't break out, your little CIA outfit could use a straight shooter." She peered into his eyes. "What you got going on?"

"I've settled on a title for my first spy novel, Phoebe."

"How about *LENNY EATS IT*?"

"You going to co-write?"

"You bet. I'll do the blood and guts scene."

Crayle relaxed. He was having some fun. "You know, the P.I. had a fantasy about you going down on him." He suppressed a chuckle.

"I am woman, Mag. I don't do that 'going down on' shit."

"At Jack's Big House. Early on. Before Hekka. When we made love …"

She took a second. "You'd lost your memories. I was just down there tying your shoe."

"Sure."

"In my work at the Bureau, I often had to remove obstacles. Your … your … your thing was in the way."

The lightweight repartee was interrupted by the sound of someone pecking at the front door security pad.

The door pushed open. Hekka staggered through the doorway, clutching two grocery bags. She kicked shut the portal, and stepped toward the kitchen.

She stopped when she saw the two. She recognized the look they both bore.

"Talking history?"

Crayle sidestepped a response. "I'd like you to use the secure tunnel to the garage, if you don't mind."

Hekka planted the bags on the kitchen counter. "You are so right. I should have parked in the garage, taken out my two bulky, heavy bags, punched in the security code, descended the narrow stairs just to get to the tunnel. Then, the hike to the end where I would ascend the second set of stairs, punch in that code, and then push the panel that would rotate the A/C unit in the kitchen, step out, and deftly place my shopping bags on the counter."

He knew his wife could perform all of the above efforts without breaking a sweat. He couldn't resist one last repartee. "You can't put a price on security."

"No, thanks," she responded.

"Which car did you take?"

"My Bronco is over at the ranch. So, I took Lenny's beloved Big Black Buick. More room than your Cobra."

"So where are the toys and other goodies for my kid. I water boarded Mag. He told me what you went for."

"How nice. Water boarding among friends. Micmac is schooled in deception if ever captured. He misled you." She provided a truly pregnant pause. "For your information, what I bought is plain old groceries. If said kid wants any of them, he needs to plop his little self out forthwith. And with respect to that, I'm ready."

"No need for the Serrano Nation to go on the warpath here."

Hekka glanced over at Phoebe. "I need to spool up some lunch before this one …" She motioned to her husband. "… goes on his own warpath."

"At least he doesn't scalp anyone."

"I'll let that pass since my scalping utensil is in the shop. Oh, I forgot something. Da—" She caught herself. "Darn. I'll be right back."

No sooner had Hekka opened the front door to step out, Micmac stepped in.

He deftly dodged her lower torso embellishment. "Hey, lady. Looking good. How about a date?"

"I'll be right back. Go inside … and behave."

CHAPTER 13

"So, my SEAL team compatriot. Pregnancies don't let you off the hook. I hear the Lipschitzes are still getting down to business. Been tending to your lady?"

"Give me a break, Mag. Alona had Lenny doin' it five times a day. Way too much. Why Phoebs and I do it …" He glanced over at her.

The Agent's mouth said nothing. Her eyes said, "Get it right!"

"Yeah," Micmac continued. "We do it precisely the perfect amount." He verified that his wife's fingers no longer caressed her Glock. "So. Another topic. On what do we spend our ill-gotten wealth?"

"Hmmm. I've heard that New Zealand is a whole bunch of beautiful."

"The Aussies might have something to say about that."

"I've heard that they and their Kiwi neighbors don't get along until there's a war. For the duration, they get down to business. Some of the best."

Crayle nodded serious agreement. "The ANZACS threw in with us in Vietnam along with the South Koreans. My father worked with some of them. And I know President Stones dad did some in-country work in Nam. Became friends with one of the Koreans. The guy and his wife live on the coast, just above San Diego."

"But, I thought *your* father was military intel."

"From the memories Doc Rorschach has restored to me, my father could walk, chew gum, shoot bad guys, and gather intel all at the same time. Tough act to follow."

"We had a few in the SEALs like that. Really, the ones you were glad were on our side."

"I believe we can add Mick MacKay to that illustrious group."

"Boy. Next time I stop by, I'll have to check my humility at the door."

"Don't listen the him, Mag. I hear about it all the time. How it was he who produced this." She stood and ran her hands about her distended belly. "He even made jokes about creating a basketball inside here, and then he wanted to have the basketball look tattooed on my tummy. With ***Micmac*** where the manufacturer name would be."

Crayle held up his hands. "Guys, guys, guys. We can all do a lot, and have done a lot. What we've just experienced tells me we should leave the humor aspect of our relationships to Lenny."

"It's right about this time when he pops in. Where is the twerp?"

"Only Alona gets to call him that. He's still back east, pursuing some old case of his father's. I'm sure he's fine, and will be hurrying back so that he doesn't miss the birth of his new baby."

"You want to see Hell To Pay. Just witness Alona going it alone, while he's goofing off on the other coast."

Micmac leaned in, as if someone might overhear. "I heard that their sex frequency is down to four per day."

Phoebe placed her finger tips to her chin. "Maybe he lied about his trip. Just to get some rest."

"I'll tell you what," Crayle said. "Let's leave Lenny alone for the rest of our conversation. Micmac, tell me about your latest gadget."

"Really wanna hear?"

"What'd I just say? My previous statement included channeling him, as well."

"All right. I'll be good. I'm working on something I've wanted to do for a long time. I finally got Langley to turn on the project and foot the bill. It's one of today's hot topics. Facial recognition."

Micmac proceeded to give him all the particulars in great technical detail. He always left it to Crayle to glean an executive level summary after such a discourse. Crayle didn't disappoint.

"I see. Your little app can find faces anywhere in the world using cutting edge technology. It then finds all others who are in any of the visuals of the targets with time stamps and locations for each. You can tell when and where for possible relationship connections."

Micmac shrugged. "I do a little research for S and T from time to time."

"You do off-the-books product development for the CIA's Science and Technology Directorate, and this new app has that aroma."

"Okay. I confess. I got a call. Wanted me to give it a field test. Before I was even finished with it."

"High priority?"

The former SEAL nodded.

"So they have a Tango in mind."

"Right. High priority."

"Who called, Micmac?"

"The president."

"Your app will need a cool name, then."

"You're right. See if you can come up with something when you're conjuring up a title for your next thriller."

"I could've used your app on the two doing the drone attack."

A second more, and he had an idea.

"I've got a name. Facial Recognition App Program. F-R-A-P."

"Hmmm."

"You'll need someone to promote it. A celebrity. Hey, remember Al Pacino? Movie star? We'll get him for the promos. Get it? FRAP Pacino?"

Micmac and Phoebe groaned in unison. Both pinched the tops of their noses as if to squelch a headache. She recovered first.

"I want Lenny back."

"Oh, another thing the president wanted. Some research on shaped charges."

"You're former UDT, Micmac. A C-4 whiz kid. You've been there and done that. It's not at all like Kimbel to waste your time."

"Yeah. C-4's my Play Doh. Look, I can't say any more right now. But think bigger. Real big."

CHAPTER 14

The next morning found the Crayles and the MacKays standing by the wing of the spy team's Falcon business jet. As they'd approached, something about the plane caught Crayle's attention.

Micmac noticed his interest, responding with a broad grin.

Crayle stepped to a long pitot tube protruding from the wing and shined his Maglight into the business end. "Since when do these wind speed collectors have rifling?"

"It's my latest."

"Let me guess. You need to feed this at 4,000 rounds per minute and, for that, you require space for all those cartridges. Of course. You reduced the in-wing fuel tanks to make room for the ammo bins."

"I was dying to tell you," Flori, the pilot, frumped, "but he threatened to put me on a No Fly List if I did."

Hekka's blood-orange Ford Bronco, fully restored, hustled into Jack's airport and slid to a stop. Hekka and Phoebe exited with a flourish.

"And where do you think you're going?" Phoebe admonished.

Hekka raised her chin as they strode toward the men. "Our babies are going to have dads, and we intend to see that it goes down that way."

"Sweetheart," Crayle parried. "We'll be right back. Lenny's gotten himself into a bind back east and, I'm sure, has overstated the situation, as usual."

"Yeah," Micmac followed. "Grossly overstated. We'll be home tomorrow. I can cut the end of that tree that pokes out onto North Shore Drive so the sheriff and his crew don't have to re-direct the traffic around it. Okay, Mag?"

"How about you stay here and get that done, and I'll go help Lenny."

"What about Alona? Why can't she go back there? It's her husband."

"I just got off the phone with her. She's got a case. In court, and all that."

Hekka had an idea. "Why don't you and I go, Magus? Phoebe can stay here until Micmac gets rid of the fallen pine tree. Then, if we're not done, they can join us. Honestly, the two of us should be able to get Lenny through whatever catastrophe he's imagined and return while you're still here."

Phoebe shook her head. "My man Micmac can work on the tree on his own. We pregnant woman must stick together. We'll have each other's backs so that there's no problem with the fronts."

"We'll keep Alona up to speed via Smartphone. Maybe a little girls on the beach time when she's able to join us."

"Right on," Phoebe concluded. "Oh. Crap. I was supposed to meet my sister, Mandy, in Vegas. Speaking of girl time."

"That's fine," Hekka said. "You could use a little recreation. We'll drop you off. Spend some time with that Delta Force sister of yours, then meet us back east in a few days. Magus and I will be fine. We can handle Lenny and, if not, Alona said she'd be finished with her case shortly, so we'll call in the cavalry if Lenny's behavior so dictates."

"Well, okay. Let's do." She kissed her husband such that he would remember that kiss. "*Adios, hombre. Mañana.*"

"Take care of yourself. That sister of yours is a wild one. Sure you can handle her in your condition?"

"Say hey, my man. I can gestate and chew gum. I'm good."

"I'm out of here," said Micmac. "Back up to the cabin. But you let me know if you need anything, Magus. Okay? Phoebe?"

"I'm optimistic. This'll be a breeze. Come on back east no matter what. We can spend a few days in the southeast, you know, eat some of that legendary fried chicken."

Micmac jumped into Crayle's red Cobra. "Oh, yeah!" He squealed off toward Highway 18 and uphill to Big Bear Valley.

As if they'd forgotten necessary protocol, Hekka and Phoebe took turns with a lean over hug with the Falcon 7X's pilot, Flori. They boarded the plane, Hekka stopping just long enough to speak to her husband. "You coming?"

Crayle shook his head and acquired a few thoughts about determined, pregnant women, then boarded.

Flori pulled the door shut, and the eclectic Crayle team subset was on its way.

• • •

An hour later, Phoebe stood alone by the wing of the Crayle team's Falcon business jet, not sure what just happened. They'd landed at Las Vegas McCarran Airport for a meet with her sister, Mandy. All as planned. But the Crayles decided to return to Big Bear with the jet. Their new plan, to help Micmac and Alona with whatever they needed, retrieve Phoebe after her romp in Las Vegas, and then, if Lenny really needed their help, they'd all go.

Flori popped her head out the doorway above. "Hate to wake you up. Need you clear of the aircraft. I must head to the gas station before I take them back."

Phoebe glanced up at Jack Sommers sexy wife. “An extra fueling stop? Did you forget to fill it up back home?”

A little laugh for each and the FBI agent made her way across the tarmac.

CHAPTER 15

It took Micmac a full hour to fly up the 18 highway in the Cobra and back to his cabin. In short order, he loaded his new invention, the razor-wire rendition of a chain saw, into the passenger seat and headed to the Crayle cabin, cleft in two by the eighty-foot pine. The garage was a separate structure and he pulled into the driveway, actuated the side-sliding garage door, and parked the sports car inside.

He was barely out of the car, when the local sheriff stood just a few feet away. The man did not appear to be happy.

"What's up, sheriff?"

"Curious layout of this property." He referred to the large log cabin with its prow-shaped windows, a smaller residence a distance away, and the separate garage structure in the middle. "Seems odd that a person would have to walk through snow to get to their car. And vice versa. Anyway, we've been looking for the owner of the smaller of these two living structures." He pointed at the Crayle cabin. "Would that be you?"

Micmac decided to omit that the layout of Jack Sommers' compound provided for two underground security tunnels, which connected the garage to the log buildings off to each side.

"No. A friend owns the place. He's away, but he asked me to come over and cut up the tree. Fire wood. Oh, and to open up the roadway, which I assume is your concern."

"My concern, and that of everyone who needs to use the road. Where, may I ask, is this owner friend?"

"Oh. That's confidential. I could tell you …"

"Very funny. Get him on the line. He's gonna have to pay for *us* to remove *his* tree."

He stepped closer and gave a thought.

"Say, don't I know you?"

Micmac knew he needed to retrace some purposefully forgotten ground. "Yes. I had a little to-do at my cabin a while back. Some folks took exception to my existence. I had to defend myself."

"Oh, yeah. I remember now. You took 'em out with one of them mini-guns. And you had a special permit from the ATF."

"Yes. And in answer to your inquiries at that time, I speed-dialed the president of the United States."

"Yes. Well. I do recall that brief little conversation." The sheriff turned on his heel. "Have a nice day." He started off, but stopped. "You say you'll remove the end that sticks over my road? No charge?"

"I'll work with your officers to assure that the problem is mitigated in short order." He pulled his razor wire saw from the front seat.

The sheriff gave it a glance. "What's that? It kinda looks like a chainsaw."

"A chainsaw?" Micmac grinned. "Cutting edge technology. Instead of saw teeth, I used military surplus razor wire. Recycled. It slices nicely through wooden objects without all the mess."

"It looks to me like something from one of them horror movies."

"As you may not know, I write training guides for the military. The one for this piece of gear states specifically, *Using this device for mayhem voids the warranty*."

"Let's see if we can clear this tree from the road. Where it passes through your friend's cabin might be a little tough, but that's your problem, not mine."

Micmac reached to shake a hand that hadn't been offered. He stepped back. "We seem to have an agreement."

The sheriff shook his head, and walked on out to his men, about half of his entire force, who were directing traffic. A few words later, he entered his sheriff's unit and drove off, still shaking his head.

Micmac smiled. The sooner he finished, the sooner he would be back with Phoebe.

He went to work.

CHAPTER 16

Lenny, former private investigator and current member of the CIA's Crayle team, continued trying to catch up with the Swiss banker, Heidi, on Hilton Head for the meet she'd commanded. He walked briskly from the Quarterdeck Restaurant to his rented Buick Enclave. His GPS guided him to an area of the same parking lot. Lenny stared at the device for a moment, then headed on foot to his destination, about 300 feet along the harbor walk from the initial restaurant.

Upon entering the newly specified restaurant, The Crazy Crab, the host seated Lenny at a good table from the P.I. or spy perspective. He could view the entire spacious restaurant, which he estimated could hold between two and three hundred patrons. As well, it afforded him a view through numerous windows to the outside deck, with seating for nearly a hundred more patrons. The wafting aromas of fresh crab legs, shrimp, and lobster reminded him of his own hunger. One patron finished his repast of bacon-wrapped BBQ shrimp with what appeared to be homemade Key Lime pie. He wondered what

Yum was in Heidi's mother tongue. His gourmet reverie was short lived.

An animal at the next table wore a cloak declaring him a *Calming Dog*. The foot-high bulldog growled at him.

"*Kalm, Blitzkrieg*," said its owner with a thick German accent. "*Kalm*."

The dog ceased, but kept a wary eye on Lenny, whose cell phone ring punctuated the moment.

He answered. He recognized Heidi's French-German accent, almost as if it was affected.

"*Bitte* … please," said his dining neighbor. She pointed outside. "Have a little respect. *Ja? Ja*."

"Just a second," Lenny said to the phone.

The bulldog farted.

"Yeah, respect," Lenny said as he jerked back from the odor.

He walked to the front door to take his call, reassessing the notion of purchasing such a beast as he headed outside.

Just outside the restaurant sat Harbour Town's boat basin. The private craft were nice, but less than beginner boats for the rich who owned second or third residences on Hilton Head.

Jarred out of his daydream, he re-engaged his phone.

"Enjoying your meal, Mr. Lipschitz?"

"Cut to the chase, sweetheart. I need to get this done and get home. I've got a baby to catch." He smiled just a bit at his approximation of a Humphrey Bogart line.

"Follow my orders to the letter, and you and your wife, Alona, shall be together shortly."

"Hey, how do you—"

"I know about her from the Dark Web. Everything is there. Don't speak. Make your way to the Best Western Ocean Breeze Inn. I chose it, because you won't be noticed there. Spend the night."

"Can't we—"

Click went his phone.

Lenny went back inside, flashed through a lukewarm repast, then drove the short distance to the hotel following his phone's GPS app.

He checked in and then took an evening walk. A narrow sand path led him past a pond and other moderate hotel properties, over a sand bank, and onto a broad, sandy beach.

The stars shone bright and plentiful. The breeze from the Atlantic refreshed him.

He sat on the pillow he'd brought from his room. After a few minutes, he rearranged himself into a prone position, stared at the stars, and fell asleep.

Lenny awoke a few hours later and knew what to do. He called Alona.

"What are you doing calling me at midnight? Isn't it 3 A.M. where you are?"

"Thought of you and our baby, that's all. I'll be back to work tomorrow and on my way home. I can't wait."

Alona shook her head. She'd married a good one.

"Get some sleep."

CHAPTER 17

With the initial Big Bear attack on their cabin behind them, the Crayles, plus Alona, headed east to help Lenny with his father's old private investigation case. At least, as far as Phoebe knew. The reality was somewhat different. She'd find that out soon enough.

In order to spend as much time with her sister as possible, she grabbed a cab. No sightseeing because the two sisters spent precious little quality time together. Mandy's Delta Force work took her away too often.

Micmac stayed home to work on the Crayle cabin, as well as his Science and Technology projects, as usual to a tight deadline.

The Wynn and Encore hotel complex was quite impressive. She'd not been here before and just the appearance of the 50 and 54 story—respectively—curved buildings took her breath away.

"Oh, this is going to be good. How Mandy got comped for this I don't know. But I'm liking it big time."

The chauffeur helped her to exit the limousine her sister had sent. Although Phoebe was quite capable, she appreciated the extras in life.

Inside the thirty-fifth floor room, Phoebe and Mandy traded hugs until Phoebe saw the floor-to-ceiling windows. "Wow, sis! Just wow!"

"Don't ask. I won't tell, anyway."

"I'm impressed. And I don't even want to know. It'd probably stress me out. I need to relax."

"And I've got just the thing. Take a seat at the table." Mandy pulled a handgun from her waist and laid it down. "You, too."

Puzzled at first, she remembered the game her sister enjoyed. She withdrew her .45 caliber Glock 30 and set it down.

"Okay, disassemble."

They pulled their weapons apart.

"Blackout goggles," said Phoebe.

Mandy pulled two from her purse. They put them on.

"They're playing your song. Love Is Blue."

"Yeah. Paul Mauriat from 1967."

"How did you, a Delta Force gal, ever get into Easy Listening?"

"Hey, the guy formed a band during WWII. Travelled Europe. Great cover for those who would spy." She gave Phoebe a sideways glance and the hint of a smile.

"Hmmm. Spies Like Us. Good name for my memoir. But, what are you doing here?"

"Simple. I needed a break from the violence."

"Enough said. Time to get down to business."

"Three, two, one, go!" said the Delta Force operative.

Both began to reassemble their firearms.

Outside in the hall, several men toting machine guns padded toward their door. Two extracted a door basher from a duffel.

The leader signaled a sixth man down the hall, who lit a full match book tied to the end of an old car antenna. He raised it to one of the ceiling sensors, then pulled the fire alarm nearby.

The two readied the device just as the two women inside both yelled, "Done!" They yanked the goggles from their heads, popped in fresh magazines, and racked their slides just as the door breached.

Bang! Bang! Bang! went Mandy's 226.

Boom! Boom! went Phoebe's Glock.

"Gun's good," Phoebe whispered.

Mandy matched her sister's inside voice. "Mine, too."

"Five down."

The women jumped up from the table and spread apart.

"I won," Mandy said.

"I reassembled first," Phoebe countered.

"I got three."

Just then, the alarm puller stepped in, expecting to find his team's targets dead.

Boom!

He fell dead. Like the other two of Phoebe's targets, a bullet between the eyes.

"Tie," the sisters chorused.

Mandy stepped over the last man standing to peek up and down the hall. "Clear!" she shouted as she pushed the man's legs aside and shut the door.

"I'd set the deadbolt, but it seems to have suffered in the scuffle." She motioned toward the room's phone. "You want to give engineering a call? And housekeeping?"

"Might be some paper work on this one. Better give Magus a heads up."

"He's got his own problems. Call our fixer. Call the president."

"Then we'll figure out what just happened."

• • •

Phoebe handled the aftermath in the usual Crayle team manner. She apprized President Stones. He quickly consulted with the Las

Vegas Police Department, which deferred immediately to the homeland security precedence. For them to keep it all quiet and affect a covert removal of the corpses posed no problem, even given a not long enough ago mass murder in Sin City. The town's economy couldn't stand much more violence of that nature. And tourists and locals alike needed to feel safe.

CHAPTER 18

Alona was as done as she could get with her judicial obligations in the Big Bear Valley. She packed her bags in a little under forty-five minutes. Five pairs of shoes would need to suffice. Another three quarters of an hour brought her to Jack's airport in a valley just northeast of the Big Bear plateau, and the always on-call Dassault business jet. With Lenny in one of his usual self-inflicted predicaments, she couldn't get to Charleston, South Carolina fast enough.

Alona landed at Charleston International Airport just before noon. She informed Flori that she might need to make another trip *today*, so the Falcon 7X headed for the refueling area reserved for private jets.

Lenny met her at the private jet gate. Within fifteen minutes, he was throwing her bag into the back of the Buick Enclave. Neither he nor Alona observed the miniature drone that hovered low outside the airport boundary. Its photographic zoom capabilities and ultra high resolution captured their likenesses quite well. If ever asked, Heidi's

IT associate, Astrid, would explain she merely wanted to ensure that Lenny and Alona were not being followed. By the wrong people.

Before they even cleared the airport, Lenny began. "If we need to spend the night, there's an Embassy Suites nearby. We'll stay there." He gave it a second. "Look. I know you're probably pissed at me, but I'm going to need legal advice. From someone I trust."

"That you trust your very own wife is a very good thing. For you."

"Yeah, uh, I wasn't exactly—what word would you use—forthcoming in our, mmmm, conversation from Hilton Head."

"It seems that your clock is winding down. Get it out. All of it. I'd hate to be representing myself on a justifiable homicide beef."

"I was probably worried about what you would say."

"Better to keep me in the dark? Boy. Your qualities just don't end at … mmm … uh …"

"Hey, I'm sorry. I took responsibility for the team's money from the diamond sale and ended up in some kind of international monetary brouhaha. Short version, I may have made a slight mistake."

"Slight being the multiplier. Am I right?"

"Crap. So, I marry a lawyer, and she sees through everything."

"A truthful statement. See to it that you're on a roll. I'd hate to have to explain to our young child what a fabulous dad you'd have made, had you lived that long."

"Ouch."

"Talk."

Lenny related a refined version of what had transpired since he'd arrived in Savannah. He left out the 'to do' at Fort Mitchell on Hilton Head. No need to frighten Alona.

He was saved from spilling all of the beans by their exit off the main highway and subsequent arrival at the confluence of Calhoun and Conrad streets.

Alona spotted a white house with a red roof. "Look at that, Lenny. A veranda on each floor. On a tree-lined street. I could … we could live in a place like that."

"Yeah. But look over there. At that orange Volkswagen with a bicycle on top. And a sign on the side. YAKIMA. I wonder what that means."

"It's a place. Southeast of Seattle, Washington. Near the nuclear place, Hanford. Where the Manhattan Project made bombs."

"Well, let's try and stay away from nuclear. I think we've had enough of that."

"Amen."

They entered into the area known as Liberty Square and knew they were close. A parking garage and a brief walk later, they arrived at the two-story Fort Sumter Visitor Education Center. Right next to the South Carolina Aquarium.

"Sightseeing?" Alona remarked as they entered an elevator.

"Supposed to go out to the fort, pick up some intel. So I was told. I did this sort of thing a bunch in my dad's P.I. company. But don't worry about anything. Check the place out. We might get a place here on the coast when this monetary issue is resolved."

She readied a repartee, but reconsidered. Support for her husband was the goal at hand.

Lenny purchased their tickets. They headed outside for the landing to board the ferry. Every time Alona would look away, he quickly scanned the environs for what Crayle and Micmac referred to as Tangos. Bad Guys to a private investigator.

The ferry, the Spirit of the Lowcountry, fell into the just large enough category. Right sized. It appeared as would an ages old side-wheeler. The bottom two decks were enclosed, the top deck open to the air. It was the best one for unobscured viewing and photographs.

They boarded and set out toward the small, man-made island of Fort Sumter. Lenny knew from a long ago history class that America's Civil War had begun there. His mind shifted to the war he seemed to have started regarding the team's funds. Hadn't his father informed him that *no good intention goes unpunished.* And that's what he'd had with respect to all that money. Good intentions.

Alona sat quietly reading an informative brochure she'd picked up while Lenny purchased tickets. "It says the fort was named after James Sumter. He was a hero of the Revolutionary War. It seems that some men just can't help themselves. You, for instance."

"Me?"

"At Mr. Lalumière's château in eastern France. How you saved the whole team, and got him arrested."

"Who'd have thought?"

"I'd have thought. And so will your new kid in a couple of weeks. I'm going to be telling him or her about his or her dad."

Just then, Lenny saw something. On the boat. Wrap-around windows permitted passengers a broad panorama from their indoor seats.

There!

He'd caught a glimpse through the forward, port side window of a youngish man with short, spiked hair. With blonde colored tips.

Then, another.

They'd found him. Worse, they'd found him with Alona. And the baby.

With no where to go, he grabbed her to him, ready to put himself in harm's way if that's what it took.

Having traversed the bow, and out of sight, the two appeared again. Through the starboard side windows.

Unaware of the circumstance, Alona struggled to free herself.

There they were! Or weren't.

An older man with a banner led several of them. The banner gave the name of a school. Teacher and students.

Lenny released Alona.

"What was that about? I like a squeeze now and then, but any harder and you would've been earning your birthing badge."

"Sorry. Just reacting to having you with me."

"Well … see over there." She pointed. "An aircraft carrier tied up at … " She paged through the pamphlet. "… Patriot's Point. The

USS Yorktown. I wish Micmac was here to see this. Let's call them, Lenny. Let's call all of them."

He hopped up. "Look. We're arriving at the dock. Let's go see Fort Sumter."

"Oh. The flag's flying at half mast."

"It speaks of life and death without saying a word."

She looked startled. "Whoa. There's a poet on board."

"Something Magus said one time."

He helped her off and up and around the parapets, and they viewed the magnificence of the southeast lowlands where they abutted the Atlantic Ocean. They enjoyed the sea breeze, which promised a brewing storm, although the turbulence pushed them around at times.

CHAPTER 19

The sub-team of Crayle, Micmac, Lenny, and Alona had arrived and *coagulated*—Lenny's term—at the ocean side Hilton Myrtle Beach Resort. The former two arrived from the Myrtle Beach International Airport in a rental SUV, while the latter pair drove up from Charleston in Lenny's rental Buick Enclave.

Crayle and Micmac announced that they were only there to support Lenny. No battle plan, no strategy, no tactics. The team had survived everything before. Each felt they would survive this operation, too.

The four took seats in the beach-facing Wet Whistle poolside bar. They chatted on and off about the weather, the beautiful beach, and the Atlantic Ocean on their doorstep. After an hour. Crayle ordered a third round of drinks. Alcohol for the men. Otherwise for the lady.

"Hi, guys." Alona popped a smile. "Before we get each other up to speed, Lenny has an announcement. Don't worry. I should really tell it, but he wants to. I'd never hear the end if I didn't let him. You're on, home boy."

Lenny cringed as if having second thoughts about exposing an embarrassment. "No, no. We're fine over here."

"You've got a problem. After all this time, I can tell," said Crayle.

"It's nothing."

"Lenny . . ."

"All right. It's Alona."

"Alona? What's wrong?"

"Oh . . ."

"Lenny."

"Well . . ."

"Lenny!"

"She's in a bit of trouble. She had this client she was defending, and they went all the way through the trial, and that's when it happened."

"What, specifically, Lenny, happened?"

"She proved him guilty."

Crayle took a moment, then said, "She can't do that."

"Yeah. She said the judge just sat there with his mouth open."

"What then?"

"The judge started to tell the jury to ignore what they'd just heard."

"And . . ."

"The foreman stood, stretched out her arm . . ." He demonstrated. ". . . and gave a big thumbs down."

"What did the judge do?"

"He turned red. He started to let 'em have it. Before he could, another jury member stood up and gave the thumbs down. Then, in clusters, the rest stood. Twelve thumbs down. Unanimous verdict."

"Probably not much precedent for a defense attorney proving her client guilty."

"No. Instead of trashing the whole thing, the judge ordered a continuance, in order to allow the Bar Association to investigate."

"It sounds like Alona set the judicial process forward a couple hundred years."

"That's my take, too. The system is supposed to bring justice. Excuse me all to Hell, but my wife did exactly that. Oh, and then the judge let the perp out."

"There's more?"

"The dude goes back to the same 7-11, and he robs it again."

"Anyone hurt?"

"Yeah. The eighty-year-old lady who owned and ran the store pulled a gun she'd bought after the first time. She shot the sucker dead."

"So now what?"

"Alona's gonna represent the old lady."

The attorney-in-question completed the thought. "Any judicial action's a ways off, and I expect that our little affair here will be tidied up presently."

Crayle ordered a fourth round.

"I believe it's our turn. We've been unable to raise Hekka and Phoebe on our phones. They should be in Wilmington, North Carolina by now. We'll keep trying."

A curious Alona asked, "What are you and your wife going to do when all of this spy fun is over?"

"I think Hekka and I will be using part of our diamond money for a place here. How about you two, Micmac?"

"Uh," Lenny interrupted. "About the money."

"What about the money?"

"It's not my fault. I saw an opportunity, that's all."

"That's not all," Alona interjected.

Lenny swung around to face her. "I hate when you take that Madam Prosecutor tone."

"You'll really dislike when I take my Swiss Army pliers to your genitals. Tell 'em!"

Lenny squirmed.

Alona reached over and grabbed his ear.

"*Ow!*"

"No secrets from prospective mama Alona or the team. Clear? And there is more, isn't there?"

"All right ..."

"All of it, Lenny, or I'll ..."

"Jeez-Louise. I said, all right." He drummed his fingers on the table, with an intense regard for them, then confessed.

"This goes back a couple of weeks. I was looking up Cryptography on my tablet. I still had an old letter from one of my father's clients. Encrypted. I wanted to decrypt it. I just typed in the first letters, Crypto, and crypto currency came up. I checked it out. Long story short, it uses technology for wealth storage and transfer. Anywhere in the world. We've run off to China one day only to wind up in France the next. My jaw dropped. Just what we need."

Micmac nodded. "I heard a little about that. Even with the transactions encrypted, there's still an opportunity for fraud, theft, and so forth."

"Let him get it all out." Alona's prosecutorial glare remained in place.

"I tracked down a resource in Switzerland. That's where everyone goes for money stuff. A banker that I shall code name Heidi. And a necessary associate, Astrid."

"We're on the same side and on the same spy team, Lenny. Code names?"

"Okay, okay. Those are their real names."

"Who's Astrid?"

"Oh. She's the IT crypto-technical expert that works closely with Heidi. We'd need her, Heidi said. What with all the fraud going on with technology, Heidi said we'd need to meet in person. That's why I'm back here."

"Nice try." Alona sounded far from satisfied. "You didn't tell this to any of us. There must be a catch."

"Silly of me to think you'd let me off the hook. I gave them our money. Then she said someone was trying to steal it, but we could foil them if I showed up and gave direct fingerprint and retina scans."

"Did you?"

"In Savannah, I met her on the paddle-wheel boat as instructed. She saw someone on the boat or on the pier, and she took off. I got a call later to meet on Hilton Head. In South Carolina. Not far from where I was."

"Where did you meet and at what time?"

"Another problem. She told me she suspected that some bad guys were following her and Astrid. She changed our meet to Charleston. Old Fort Sumter."

Alona stayed on the prosecutorial tack. "Mr. Lipschitz, what happened on Hilton Head that you left out?"

"Jeez-Louise. All right. The day after I called you, she directed me to the Fort Mitchell ruins on the north side of the island. Said to go into the Old Fort Pub restaurant next door and order a drink and some food. She specified it as if no one else would order the strange combination. Dry vodka shaken-not-stirred martini with a twist, along with a bowl of She-Crab soup. I did. She called again. Said to go over to the fort ruins and walk around. I did. That's when I saw them."

"Saw who?"

"The ones with the crew cuts. The tops of the hair prongs sticking up were all colored green."

Alona drew closer. "How many men did you personally observe, Mr. Lipschitz?"

"Four. They pulled submachine guns. Silenced submachine guns."

"You weren't going to tell us this little fact? I'm thinking death penalty if you do that ever again. What then?"

"Hey, I was concerned for you and the kid. That you might worry. Look, Heidi hadn't been completely honest with me. Probably thought I'd stress out. I read her out for not warning me. She apologized. That's when she directed me to Charleston. To Fort Sumter. She said it would be easy to spot anyone going or coming since access was all by ferry. She was sure we could meet and safely transact our business."

"You can tell us how you managed your way out of four submachine guns versus your flaccid little Walther PPK. Another time. When I'm not so pissed."

"Let's get it over with. There are several earthen berms at Fort Mitchell. One of the Greens moved sideways to have a straight shot at me. He stepped past a sign. Boom! Unexploded ordnance from long ago. Took 'em all out. I exited the scene. Stage right."

Alona remained pissed. "I think we'll skip the rest of the trial phase, and go straight to sentencing."

Crayle jumped in. "So, Lenny, what's the status of our money … and what do we do next?"

Next to him, Micmac kept pecking at his Smartphone. "I still can't reach Phoebe and Hekka. I have plenty of bars, but no connection in Wilmington. I'm sure they're okay. I'd just like to hear them say so."

"Roger that, my friend."

Lenny's Smartphone rang.

A voice, Heidi's voice, mentioned just four words. The next location.

• • •

The four headed back to the parking garage, set the GPS on Micmac's phone. They could have used the one on Crayle's SUV, but it would leave a trail. They avoided trails at all costs.

The route was brief. They arrived at the Broadway At The Beach center in fifteen minutes. A short walk from the parking lot, and they entered an expansive area chock full of retail stores, restaurants, and various other venues of entertainment. A huge man-made pond centered the area.

Alona scanned the scene. "This place looks great for tourists like us, as well as the locals, doesn't it, Lenny?"

"It sure does, love. Check out the power boat ride on the lake. Two tiny boats with huge engines. Sounds like the roar of one of those Navy fighters."

Crayle watched the boats load up on a dock to their left, and then fairly fly across the water to their right.

"Hey," said Lenny. "I saw a Margaritaville on the way in. It's five o'clock somewhere, so I'll take Alona and we can do margaritas while I wait for the next call from Heidi."

"Alona is pregnant, Lenny. She can't drink."

"She can have one of those Virgin-ritas. You guys coming?"

"Approaching nine months along, I think we can stipulate that I'm not a virgin, darling."

"Don't I know." Lenny admired his nails. Then, "Oh! I believe I just stepped on a pop-top!"

Alona punched his shoulder.

"Ouch! So I marry the female rendition of Rocky." He turned to the other men. "You guys coming?"

"That's okay," Crayle said. "Micmac and I will stick around here. In case any of those color-spiked hair friends of yours come around."

Lenny and Alona headed off. Crayle and Micmac waited until the other two were safely inside their restaurant.

"Let's check out the Hard Rock Café, Magus. It's right over there." He pointed.

At that moment the two power boats, each with a pilot and a passenger, stopped in the center of the lake. Pointed their way.

The pilots hit the throttles. Their passengers pulled compact weapons from what Jack Sommers labeled Go Bags.

The roar of the engines echoed heavily off of the flat store fronts. They covered the unsilenced rounds being fired.

Crayle and Micmac ducked.

"Orange hair!"

"Team Two, I'm guessing."

"We've got universal Consummate Concealed Carry authorized by President Stones himself. Let's do it!"

They spread themselves ten feet apart, lifted, and fired.

Like a fire drill that was anything but Chinese, tourists and spectators alike scrambled, sometimes fought, for cover.

On Micmac's side, the gun-toting passenger was unsighted. He took the driver instead.

Crayle put four rounds in the other passenger as the boat started a turn to avoid hitting the cement side of the lake.

The other boat, its driver now quite dead, slammed into the lake rim and exploded in a fireball. The passenger flew skyward in flames like a man-sized, Fourth of July firework. Unknown to him, his return flight into the water squelched his fire.

The whole affair scattered the large crowd in a pedestrian version of the vaunted Chinese Fire Drill. Because the Crayle and Micmac weapons were silenced, no one noticed their part in the fracas. They re-holstered, and headed to the Hard Rock.

• • •

Forty minutes later, while the Broadway At The Beach shopping mall swarmed with police, SWAT teams, the local FBI agent, and a fire brigade, the four returned to their Myrtle Beach hotel.

Due to the danger of being spotted and taken down by law enforcement, the ride back to the hotel seemed much longer than the ride out.

They did arrive safely and trudged as quickly as possible to their rooms. Despite having put away three of the Margaritaville Uptown Top Shelf margaritas, Lenny felt wired. It took Alona's hand clamped over his mouth to shut him up and not draw attention.

When they stepped into the Crayle room, he observed that a modicum of levity can accompany the insane occurrences that just transpired. "Have a couple of drinks there, Lenny?"

"Just another one of my sacrifices. Alona can't drink. I was drinking for two."

Alona added her own take. "The drinks will wear off quickly. That's not the problem. It's all the Volcano Nachos he gorged himself on that I'll have to deal with later."

The crew shared a brief chuckle. Crayle, as was his wont, asked for intel. Especially since the Lipschitzes hadn't witnessed the gun battle and speed boat air burst. "Anything special that got your attention."

Lenny shrugged, then continued with his Margaritaville experience. "Man, we heard a commotion outside. People were running to windows. They missed the volcanic eruption Warren Buffett has going on in there. Spectacular."

"It's Jimmy Buffett, Lenny. There were some fireworks outside, too. Nothing like the volcano."

"I see you both got yourselves Hard Rock tee shirts. We missed out, but the volcano was worth it."

"Let's all of us get some sleep. It's been a long day. If Heidi calls, set up a meet tomorrow. Micmac and I will find some time to see if we can track our two Swiss bankers."

"The app is still young," Micmac added. "But it's the app we have, so yes."

CHAPTER 20

Prior to their departure to help Lenny, Micmac busied himself removing the blown over, eighty-foot pine tree. Crayle dealt with the cabin rebuild codes and regulations. It seemed the local politicians did not appreciate receiving orders from the White House. They slow-walked every request. The cabin reconstruction required momentous code changes, they said. It should have an attached garage, they said.

Phoebe called Hekka.

With their kitchen destroyed, Hekka Crayle travelled all the way to Sandy's Sports Bar and Restaurant for a to-go order of their delicious fish and chicken tacos. Normally, she would have pulled her blood orange Bronco off the road to take the call. But, thanks to gadget man, Micmac, she just said, "Answer."

Phoebe's voice sounded a little too animated. "I need your help."

"Something's wrong? Water break?" She waited. "Lenny?"

"Good guess. The twerp's back east on some gig left over from him and his father's P.I. business. He's already dragged in Alona. Before she flew out, she read me in."

Phoebe related the substance of her talk with Lenny's wife.

After a moment to consume the new intel, Hekka responded. "I picked up sandwiches, potato salad, and cole slaw for the guys. I'll drop off their lunch, then swing by to pick you up. That work?"

"So, you're in?"

"Myself and the baby are in."

"Fabulous. I'll notify Jack's airport. Flori will take care of the rest."

"Pack light.

"Right. This is going to be quick, right after I kill that little—"

"Ah, ah," Hekka admonished. "No foul language. Our babies are listening."

"Yeah. See you in twenty."

• • •

Phoebe and Hekka arrived at the Wilmington, North Carolina airport. While trooping through the terminal, Phoebe apprized Hekka that Alona, who never asked anyone for help, had asked Phoebe. She'd described how Lenny was being led north along the coast from Savannah, Georgia, and that a trend had developed. From that, she picked Wilmington as a safe spot ahead of the apparent path to apprehend the errant P.I., and then use the hotel room as a base of operations.

• • •

The hotel they chose, almost at random, was perfect. The Best Western Plus Coastline Inn exceeded expectations. The room window framed old wooden docks below, the glistening Cape Fear River, and on the other side, sat battleship USS North Carolina. It would seem perfectly natural to pull up a couple of chairs to await the sunset. Especially with almost nine months of pregnancy under their belts. But not Hekka and Phoebe.

It was early evening and there the two stood, outside their hotel, with nowhere to go, nothing to do, and no one but themselves with whom to do it.

Just twenty feet away stood a couple of horses attached to a four-wheeled carriage. No point looking for a bar, not with babies on board. A carriage ride would do just fine until they heard from Lenny.

The driver gave a running monologue as he ordered forth the horses. On this side you have this, and on that side you have that. By force of habit, Phoebe continuously scanned the periphery. Looking for anyone who looked suspicious. She smiled at herself. "Relax," she said.

Just as she did, a man stepped out of a phone booth not twenty yards to their left. His long overcoat seemed a bit much for such a nice Southern evening, until its purpose became clear.

He yanked an assault weapon from its hiding place, and pointed it her way.

Phoebe yelled, "Driver! Make 'em run!"

The driver's head spun to see which of his charges had emitted the annoyance, and he saw the gunman. He snapped the reins with all of his strength. The horses dawdled, not at all inspired to action.

Phoebe ducked, pulling Hekka down with her.

The round of gunfire buzzed overhead, hitting the driver in the back and killing him instantly.

He fell forward onto the horses. They spooked.

There they were. In downtown Wilmington, North Carolina. Two quite pregnant women in a runaway horse carriage with someone firing an automatic weapon at them. This was not in the guide book.

The horses exploded into grid-locked traffic. One reared up, coming down with both hooves on a gold Prius. Its roof caved, exploding the rear window. Screams sounded from horrified bystanders on sidewalks and in street-side cafés.

A drizzle began and filtered into the hybrid car's damaged batteries. Sparks arced. So intense, they could be seen from several blocks away.

Phoebe jumped from the carriage and, as she reached for Hekka, reassured her baby that things were going to be fine.

A car screeched behind. The same killer jumped from the passenger seat and took aim, underestimating the North Carolina locals. They jumped him and yanked his driver from the car. They proceeded to administer southern justice as Phoebe and Hekka fled the scene.

Hekka was already clicking her Smartphone off. "They're on the way!"

Seconds later, five police officers arrived on bicycles, took custody of the perps, recorded basic witness information, then looked around for the intended victims.

Gone.

CHAPTER 21

The Lipschitzes had left Crayle and Micmac and returned to their room. Quick to bed, they slept like babies for hours. Shortly after they awakened, Lenny sat at the desk, working his tablet computer detachable keyboard and alternately pecking on the device's touch screen. He scanned for notable world events, stopping at one on China and its new empress. It happened when he turned to inform his wife.

The belt flew over Lenny's head, then snapped hard against his chest. A quick cinch behind pinned his arms. Lenny heard his captor's light steps as she walked around him.

"Now that I have you alone, I don't need to worry about all of those annoying constitutional protocols. I read up on KGB techniques, so I can employ those should you be holding anything else back."

"This sounds like one of those sex games. Do what you gotta do. Just make sure that I get off in the end."

"It's true. We've played before. This time will be non-sexual. A plain old interrogation."

"Let me go. I confess." He laughed. "What is this all about?"

"The Sammy project thing you tried on everyone didn't fly. Did it? We're going to squeeze any last drops of truth this time. To set the proper mood, pretend we're inside the basement of the KGB's Lubyanka Prison in the 1970's. In Moscow."

"You're a defense attorney. You think you can pull off the Madam Prosecutor bit?"

"Is the Pope a Catholic?"

"I'm not sure anymore. After recent events."

Alona extracted from him every last bit of the Swiss money situation. How he'd initially hooked up with and vetted the two Swiss women. She finished feeling less confident than ever that they'd get their money access situation resolved. She also noted that, again and again, she found it necessary to remind herself that the baby inside needed a father.

No sooner had she removed the restraint, than Lenny got Magus Crayle on the phone, and asked for a meet. Now.

• • •

Fifteen minutes later, Lenny strolled the wide, sandy beach with Crayle and Micmac. While out in the open with numbers of people randomly placed in beach chairs, in the surf itself, or strolling like themselves seemed like the last place for confidential conversations, that wasn't always the case.

With the noise of the surf, with the sound of the children, and with the only authority, the lifeguards, clearly visible, the choose-your-environment technique sufficed to keep any prying ears at bay.

Lenny slurped an HCL—Hyper-Caffeine Latte—he'd ordered from his room and picked up at the restaurant. He glanced over at Micmac with a gleam in his eye. The former UDT expert responded.

"Alona has probably gone through her bag of tricks to squeeze the last drop of intel from you by now. Fortunately for me, and not for you, we performed and experienced some rather harsh interrogation techniques at the SEAL evasion school on San Diego's Coronado Island. You already told us you've sold our one-pound bag of flawless, one-carat diamonds for cash that you stashed in a Swiss bank. And some assorted details. After all this time, I know that look right there. What else is there, P.I.?"

"Here's the full story. Stop me if I tell you anything new."

He glanced at the other two. Not a word.

"The one-pound bag of diamonds came from the Frenchman, Sylvain Lalumière, who laundered mid-east water priority money via Jean-Marc's friend, and my half brother, Wolfie, the diamond broker. Those two had been school mates at the University of Leiden. That's the connection. Lalumière's son, Jean-Marc, then delivered it to the international finance middleman, Xiang, in Kaohsiung. That's in Taiwan. Southwest."

"We know. Go on," Crayle said.

"Quickly," Micmac added.

"The bag paid for those little nuclear bombs for Lalumière. But Crayle team, us, jumped on Jack's jet plane, descended on Xiang in Kaohsiung, and relieved him of it. Upon request from my brother Wolfie's old diamond firm—after his death at the hands of Pattie Norbrunn—I travelled to Amsterdam, and took the bag with me. I then sold the bag to someone via this Heidi person. I'm sure that the recipient bought the bag in order to purchase something nefarious from some other criminal. Don't have a clue on the last two items."

"Sure. The use of cutouts to hide or masquerade the purpose and the end user is a necessity on the international dark side."

"Yeah, but that cuts both ways. Whoever's at the other end of the chain doesn't know about me or about Team Crayle." He waited to no avail. "Nicely done, Lenny," he concluded.

"Sorry I missed my cue. Fine job. All we need now," Crayle mused aloud, "is global access on an immediate, untraceable, failsafe funds transfer mechanism."

Lenny's smug grin had them gulping their own drinks, and wishing for a shot of something stronger.

"I've bought us into just the thing. Does everything you mentioned. Ah." He tweaked his chin. "I'm probably just wasting my time." He drummed his fingers on the paper cup.

Micmac headed for the edge. "Lenny, listen to me. Tell us what you have or I will personally demonstrate, on you, the latest enhanced interrogation techniques, short hairs and all."

"Jeez-Louise, UDT guy! Okay. Okay. It's called CrapCoin. It uses that Blockchain transaction technology—tried and proven."

"Put away your torture devices, Micmac. I know a bit about the crypto-currency technology. It's based on sound mathematical principles."

"It is? Shoot. No torturous interrogations today. Damn."

"CrapCoin?"

"Yeah. Clever, eh? Informed sources told me they call it that so no one other than an elite few—Gordon Gekko types, politicians, fake Liberals, fake Conservatives—who know that it's real, and that it's the best, will use it. Not even the FBI can break in."

"I'll check with Phoebe on that."

"No! No! No! No one must know. Just the immediate team."

CHAPTER 22

Directed by the sultry and mysterious Swiss banker, Heidi, the crew of Magus Crayle, Mick MacKay, and Lenny and Alona Lipschitz drove their two rental cars all the way from South Carolina's Myrtle Beach to a town that, without the team's experiences over the past two years, would have seemed inappropriate. Kill Devil Hills. North Carolina. It sat on the long and skinny Outer Banks strip of island territory, which seemed to dangle like a thread from the southeast corner of Virginia, and it was no stranger to mobs of tourists each Summer.

They checked into two rooms at the Sea Ranch Resort. The hotel sat just off the beach and the splashing Atlantic Ocean. Even though a severe storm had battered its way across the deep south, it would pass over this site and head out to sea to dissipate over night. They'd be quite safe in the hotel, barring any major roof leaks. A perfect setting for drinks by the fireplace, they enjoyed the drinks and the fireplace, but retired early. A great deal had happened along the southeastern seaboard, and they were exhausted. None heard the heavy rain that night. Or what it portended.

• • •

The next morning, Lenny and Alona left the others of the team a message at the front desk. It read, "Storm passed last night out to sea. We're headed south to Hatteras. We're taking a break. Alona wants to see the lighthouse."

"Translation," Crayle said after he'd listened to the message on his room phone. "Lenny is taking the Ferals away from the rest of us."

Before he could proceed further with his conjecture, his Smartphone interrupted all thought patterns of the two men. It was the special ring. The one reserved for their wives.

They proceeded with a verbal handshake for safety's sake, and then with the content. Crayle informed them of the many attempts to contact them and received a 'ditto' from the other end. He went on to provide a sitrep status of Lenny's efforts, but left out the violence. He'd worried at the time that, no matter the incredible strength of these two women, they didn't need additional stress and worry heaped on them so far into their pregnancies. Last, he informed them of their current hotel, and about the Lipschitzes traipsing off south along the Outer Banks to the world famous Hatteras Lighthouse. Having left out the men with the colored hair at Broadway At The Beach, he also omitted his theory that Lenny intended to draw them away. He recalled something his mother had told him over and over. Always tell the truth. All of it. In this particular instance, he wished he had.

In their Wilmington hotel room, Hekka shook her head as she glanced over at Phoebe. "That's no good. He took Alona."

"More like she wouldn't let him out of her sight. She's determined that their baby is going to have a father, alive and kicking."

• • •

Before the Lipschitzes cleared the driveway that morning, Alona fell asleep. Twenty minutes later, she awoke.

"Oh. Where are we?"

She checked outside. The rain was gone, but Lenny was plodding the car at a snail's pace through nine inches of water left by the recent storm.

"What are you doing?"

"Heading south to the lighthouse. That's what you wanted to see."

"Don't be putting this on me, home boy. You should have used your intellect and determined that this was a bad idea. What if the car stalls out? And I go into labor?"

"Babies have been delivered by fathers before. I'm good."

"What if those hair-colored maniacs track us to the lighthouse?"

"They'd have the same problems we're having."

"If something happens to me … our baby … "

"It's far enough along … "

"That it might survive? It might be delivered somehow and live?"

"I shouldn't have said—"

"Without you and me? Won't happen that way. I'm hereby willing us to survive any and all mayhem. Or worse."

"And I second that motion." A quick smile and a high five.

"But what you just said. If something awful happened to us, our baby would survive. That, my love, is Jewish strong. If I … you know … "

"So choosing the scalping option with Hekka is no longer an option?"

"Her Serrano ancestors have provided other means should you mess up."

"Point taken. I'll try … " He glanced over at her. "… I'll see to it that I don't mess up."

• • •

Later that morning, Crayle met Micmac for breakfast in the Beachside Bistro at their hotel. They both ordered the single biscuit and gravy, which they washed down with 'real' coffee.

"Large portions of good food, reasonably priced. This restaurant is homey inside," Crayle observed. "Medium blue on a well-lit interior. Outside dining, if you like."

"I'm a sailor. I'd like to sit here watching the surf. And out to the horizon."

"All that growth on top of the sand dune keeps the sea breeze from blowing sand in our food."

"We former SEALs use the sand instead of floss and toothpaste."

They shared a brief laugh.

"We both look a little worried, my gritty SEAL friend. With reason. Our pregnant women are down there in Wilmington, and Lenny and Alona have buzzed off south. To some lighthouse. In flood waters. What's your take?"

Micmac massaged his chin where a few whiskers had escaped the blade for a few days. "I think the Lipschitz duo will be fine. I think our wives have probably shopped the town dry. And I think our wives don't have a clue what has happened along the way. To us."

"This Heidi seems to be on the run from whomever keeps showing up and trying to do everybody in. The hair cuts and the colors don't track with anything I've experienced. Or remember that I've experienced."

"That much money can attract a crowd of bad people."

"The value of a pound bag of diamonds was around $9,000,000 a year ago. Inflation's been pretty bad. Probably a lot more now. People around the globe use precious commodities to store their wealth. Whatever an ounce of gold or a perfect one-carat diamond bought before can buy the same thing regardless of inflation, or even deflation. Doesn't matter … wait." Crayle answered his phone.

Lenny.

"Say, boss. It's me. We're at Hatteras. The lighthouse place."

"Through how much standing water?"

"Piece of cake. I drove. Anyways, just got a call from our financial friend. Heidi. She heard about the fireworks on the news, and has hightailed it out of the area. She'll get back to me in the next few days, but she sounded afraid. Bankers don't do stuff like we do. What's SOP for us could be SOL for them."

"Well, I'm glad they're safe. I think Micmac and I'll stop off at Kitty Hawk. Check out the origin of manned flight and all. I'll get Hekka and Phoebe on the phone. That'll be some update. At least they're safe."

"Good enough, my man. Just a second. Alona wants a picture of her and the baby in front of the lighthouse. Catch you later."

Click.

"A man of few words. Come on, Micmac. Kitty Hawk. Let's check out."

• • •

A half hour later, the two men checked out and headed to Kitty Hawk. Although they had their GPS, the route was well marked with Wright Brothers National Memorial signage.

They arrived at the site to be greeted by two separate ingress lanes, each with its own small gray guard house.

Once in the parking lot, Micmac pulled a couple of walking sticks from the car's trunk, and the two worn out men trudged to a large square building that appeared to be a museum of sorts. Inside sat an exact replica of the Wright brothers plane.

"They must've been short," Micmac said. "You and I on there, and that fine craft couldn't get off the ground, engine or no."

Crayle browsed the walls.

"Check out these portraits. Famous people."

"Here's one of Charles Bolden. Major General Charles F. Bolden, Junior. First African-American astronaut, it says. Appointed NASA Administrator for a while. Whew! And all that after he'd earned a masters degree at USC. I'm surprised he didn't captain a National Championship-winning football team in his spare time."

"Let's get out there and imagine what it was like all those years ago."

They walked outside to see a flat grassy field with several vertical, white stones, distance markers, one denoting the end of each pass.

"Let's head over there to the left, Micmac. I believe that little hill is where they took off."

"I'd hate to be the ones who dragged the plane up that hill."

A hundred yards later, they'd climbed a number of steps to mount the hill, then turned to survey the landscape. A full-scale metal reproduction of the Wright Brothers aircraft sat there along with several metal statues of those who'd been involved.

At an adjacent white building, next to a hidden civilian runway marked First Flight Airstrip, four men stepped outside.

"No vehicles," said the leader. "I've been instructed to take them alive. Ha! They're to be considered as CIA and SEAL dangerous. To the extreme. Double time to get them surrounded. Then we move in. No collateral casualties are our orders. But the two men on top. They gotta die."

While Micmac moved a little left, then right, looking to where he might have taken off, Crayle surveyed the green landscape surrounding their lookout point. It commanded a grand view of the territory.

He grabbed the former SEAL by the collar, dragging him behind a life-size statue of the flight-pioneering brothers.

There were only a few other visitors to the site given the time of year, and the just-passed major storm. Those who saw what transpired next fled toward the parking lot.

Shots pinged off the statue. Crayle and Micmac stayed safe while two assassins fired and the other two attempted to circle around behind.

"I'm hoping to hell you're armed."

"Don't mention hell, please. Here, pull the bottom off the walking stick. Like this."

Crayle watched, then did the same.

"It's a point and shoot technology. Not too accurate at range."

"Good thing they're close. And getting closer. How—"

"Use your thumb on the other end. It takes a little practice."

"I was afraid of that."

"We'll take the two coming around first. That way, the statue will keep us covered."

"Dibs on the one nearest me."

"I always get sloppy seconds."

The two killers circling assumed their targets to be unarmed. Especially in a government park.

Crayle fired first. It took him a second to remove his thumb. Holding produced automatic fire.

Micmac fired second, but scored first, having had practice at the Big Bear target range.

Then Crayle's man went down.

The other two, wanting to live and fight another day, turned and fled. In a few minutes, the roar of their light plane's engine wafted over the hill and past the bullet-riddled statue.

"They're outta here. Man, did you see what I saw?"

"Yeah. Blue tinged flattops. Same army, different squad."

Next they heard sirens. A long way off, but closing fast.

"We'll skip the gift shop," Crayle said as the two ran down the launch hill and to the parking lot.

A park ranger stopped them as they loaded the walking sticks into the interior of their car via the hatch.

"Did you men hear or see something? Almost sounded like gunfire."

Crayle, resourceful spy, answered the uniformed and armed ranger. "Yeah. We heard something, too. Over there by the airstrip. I thought I heard someone cry out, but wasn't sure. You'd better check it out. Can't have bad stuff happening on government property. Especially sacred ground like this."

"Okay. I'll check it out. You two stay right here. I'll need to talk to you some more."

"Yes, sir," Micmac said, betraying his military background.

The man took off. Crayle and Micmac did the same just a short time later.

"We have our luggage so no need to return to the hotel. Head us out of here."

"You bet, Magus. Gone in far less than sixty seconds."

As Micmac sped them away, Crayle's phone rang.

"Hi."

"Magus, where have you been? We've been trying to reach you all since we landed. Could've used some help here."

"All's fine at this end. We've just been goofing off. And you?"

"We'll talk when we see you. Are you coming down here to Wilmington?"

"Uh, no. We'll do a meet."

He provided new GPS coordinates. She repeated them back.

"See you in a couple of hours. Oh, I'll call Lenny and read him in on the new plan. See you there."

"Bye. And love. Times two."

He heard Phoebe in the background.

"Times four."

CHAPTER 23

The team members, now all able to track as well as call each other, affected a simultaneous arrival. Exhausted. They trooped their luggage to pre-assigned rooms at the Williamsburg red brick and white trimmed Country Inn. By prearrangement, they assembled in the Crayles' room rather than just flop on their beds. Exhausted.

"I'm beat," Lenny said. "Can we make this short?"

Phoebe tilted her head to one side. "You don't shut up, I can make your life short." She observed Alona's belly for a couple of seconds. "Sorry, Alona. Lenny and I have this thing."

"As long as it doesn't involve *his* thing, we're good."

"Relax, everyone." Crayle took the helm. "Exhale. They have an indoor pool. Breakfast is included. And so is a happy hour. Every day." He glanced around. "Consider it. De-stress."

Micmac observed. "Crayle assumes command. Take it away, Magus … Sir."

After a pregnant pause, the team members smiled. Each glanced around at the others, heads nodding up and down. They all relaxed back into their seats.

"I put in a call this morning to Jack. He's still at Manassas HQ. He arranged our lodging. Working class accommodations to keep us properly grayed out. And comped, of course. I thanked him." He glanced across at the P.I. "I'm certain Lenny wants to thank us all for helping him with his project at quite lethal risk to life and limb."

Lenny started his mouth. Quick, Alona leaned to him. In that instant, she wrapped one hand over his mouth, while the other clamped the back of his head, forcing an acquiescent nod.

"Thank you, Lenny," said Crayle. "When I spoke with Jack, I told him about our little quasi-op here in the American southeast."

"What'd he say?" Hekka wanted to know.

"He told me to stay safe, and then reminded me of my commitment to one President Kimbel Stones."

"Oh, the CIA thing."

"Yes. The CIA thing." He allowed a weary shake of his head, then added, "Let's all catch some sleep. Micmac can do his reveille thing in the morning, then we're off for a terrific breakfast. I know just the place."

Alona relaxed her grip on Lenny so she could get up and head to her room. She and the baby really needed a good night's sleep.

Unencumbered, Lenny piped up. "You said earlier they include breakfast at this place. Let's eat here tomorrow."

"Daybreak in the lobby, team. Trust me, Lenny. You'll love my selection. Don't dally, though. Post breakfast we'll have time for independent couples R and R. Late afternoon, we'll meet up at Richmond International Airport for our ride home. It's a joint use, military-civilian field, so don't get excited when you see the hardware."

Lenny wasn't finished. "The 7X only has one bedroom."

"We'll take turns. It's that … or walk."

"Whine."

• • •

The next morning, Micmac made the rounds rousting his team mates. A number of complaints and a half an hour later, the three window-tinted, black Denali SUV's caravanned 12.9 miles on the Colonial Parkway to the modern version of colonial Yorktown.

Crayle knew the area quite well. He played travel guide via a secure intercom system.

"This is the confluence of the York River and the Chesapeake Bay outlet to the Atlantic. The beach alongside, as you can see, is not as filled in the Autumn as it is in the Summer."

"Small wonder they named this here road Water Street." Lenny glanced around for acknowledgment of his wit. To no avail.

Crayle, quite practiced at ignoring the P.I., continued. "It's a little chilly."

The team observed a few sunbathers and felt they could also see a multitude of goose bumps on each. All fully understood the notions of determination, persistence, and fortitude.

"The high, arching bridge you see just to our west can take you to the Virginia end of the Maryland peninsula. Sounds a bit strange, but that's how they laid it out."

"And that warship being towed into the river mouth over to your right," Micmac interjected, "is a Landing Ship Dock type, used by the Gator Navy." He observed the puzzled looks. "The Navy's amphibious forces."

"Thanks for the help, Micmac. And across the street is the Yorktown Beach. Come on. Let's get inside and get some food."

"Give a second, Mag. Watch that tall bridge."

They did.

As the Navy ship approached, a major section pivoted to provide access up the Chesapeake Bay to the ship. An amazing feat of engineering.

"Micmac, that may be the ultimate gadget."

"Have you forgotten? I'm the gadget man. And I'm not done yet."

They entered the pub.

• • •

The Yorktown Pub was very bistro-like, as its name would indicate. Inside, twelve U.S. Army soldiers occupied a long table and seemed to be enjoying an off-base Saturday meal. Crayle noticed their shoulder patches. He knew where they were stationed. Knew it well, in fact.

The meal proved excellent, as Crayle knew it would. "Okay. Take a potty break. I'll meet you out front. As I said last night, we're headed off in our own direction. A little couples time. I've placed suggested destinations in your glove boxes, but you can go almost anywhere using your vehicle's GPS. But, meet Hekka and I at the Richmond airport at 6 P.M. sharp." He glanced at the former sailor. "1800 hours. At that point, we're headed home. Sound good. Go!"

They all headed for the johns except Phoebe. She moved over next to Crayle.

"You've had that look in your eye, Magus Crayle, since we reached the hotel. What are you up to?"

"No use telling a lie, I suppose."

"Actually, I'm still FBI. Lying to me would be a federal crime."

He leaned over and whispered in her ear. She pulled back.

"Woohoo. If you've got an extra, I'll do Quantico! Just inscribe it to the FBI. Include FIDELITY–BRAVERY–INTEGRITY in whatever you write. That motto, my dear friend, is non-negotiable."

"I have an extra copy. In the back of your Denali. Hidden behind a side panel. So, it's a deal." He smiled. "You know, we've known each other a long time, haven't we?"

"Yes, we have. And that early knowing, before you met Hekka, that's in the bible." She returned his smile.

"If God only knew."

CHAPTER 24

Lenny and Alona were first out of the Yorktown Pub and first back to their vehicle.

"That was good," Alona allowed. "You know I like being around the others. I can't imagine any better friends to have."

"Yes, and we're all going to have new babies shortly, and all participate in their upbringing. I can't wait."

"There could be no better influences. Magus is like the old TV series, I Led Three Lives. Only, he didn't know it. 'Til recently. Hekka with her Serrano Indian heritage. That kid is going to have the world by its tail."

"Yeah, but what about that Micmac? A Navy SEAL. And an underwater demolitions and weapons specialist. And Phoebe the Fibbee. That kid will definitely be a straight shooter."

"Then there's us. Holy crap! Our kid will be a cross between a private investigator and an attorney."

"May God help us all."

They both enjoyed a good laugh.

"You know, when I retire from this intel stuff, I'm going to hand down my Walther PPK."

"We need out of the violence business, dear heart. For us and for our kids, plural. And if we don't, the word could be bequeath."

• • •

Micmac and Phoebe headed outside right after the Lipschitzes. He removed his wind breaker and wrapped it around his wife's shoulders.

"Thanks. It is chilly. So besides wreaking havoc wherever you go, you SEALs are gentlemen. You learn that at the school on Coronado?"

"Certainly not in foreign bars. Uh … food and beverage establishments."

"I'll let you go on that one. What struck you most about the pub?"

"You'll laugh."

"I'll do worse if you continue to pull a Lenny."

"All right. Okay. It was the bathroom."

"The bathroom. Seriously? Great food. Great service. Salt air wafting in. The bathroom?"

"Yeah. It was the floor tiles."

"I am, by my gender, unfamiliar with the Men's Room environment. We ladies sit … for both versions of elimination. And you're telling me you whiz on the floor tiles?"

"Have all the fun you want. It just so happens that these floor tiles had inlays of crabs. Not real ones. Artistic ones."

"Well, I hereby promise that I will never be crabby, and perhaps we'll have some of those tiles when we remodel our own bathroom back at the cabin. Hmmm?"

"I believe that I just heard the R word. Oh, Phoebs, look over there … "

• • •

Magus and Hekka were the last to head out. They thanked the staff inside and offered an extra twenty dollars, which they declined. All gave them a vigorous wave as they left, as though they were rock stars.

"It's time for a little confession. The pub was suggested from our unofficial travel agent from Nova Scotia. I think we owe him for that. What do you suggest?"

"Nova Scotia is still in Canada, right?"

"Yes. It's apparently a portion of the French crowd in Quebec that has wanted to secede from the Dominion. If you look at Nova Scotia on a map, you can imagine it as an exclamation point on the whole country."

"Nicely done, Mr. Crayle. Nicely done."

"Now that we've established that, I'm thinking beer."

"I've heard they have Alcoholic Beverage Control stores in Canada. True?"

"True. ABC is the old name. They're called LCBO officially. It's a government agency put in place to assure that Canadians drink enough of the health-giving liquid."

"No wonder they look so healthy."

"And with that bit of levity, we're out of here."

He fired up the Denali, and pointed them west, intending no further adventures like the ones before. Neither one of them kidded themselves. They knew from experience.

Best intentions shared common ground with best laid plans.

CHAPTER 25

The former CIA heads, DCI and DDCI, had been confined to Supermax in Colorado due to their discovered connections to the ultra secret society, Illuminé. There the CIA's lead head doctor, Rorschach, reprogrammed the DCI and the DDCI and returned them to Langley before the mini-nuclear bomb attack by Chin's daughters.

Their seventh floor offices at the CIA's Langley headquarters had been the first to be destroyed due to the overhead air burst. Based on the intel presented to him, all President Kimbel Stones could determine was that the fate of the two leaders was unknown. Aware that the agency above all others required unabated direction, especially in the most dire of circumstances, he followed the *Failover Protocol* and transferred operational control to Jack Sommers. His office far beneath the old Manassas battlefield was distant enough from Langley to have been shaken, but not stirred.

Jack was already standing in as head of the Office of Specialized Staffs, OSS, due to the demise of one Neil Wohlford at the hands of one Pattie Norbrunn. Jack still ran the Strategic Solutions Office,

SSO, under the OSS, while he continued to manage the International Operations Unit, IOU, which referenced the Crayle team. He'd approached the president with a notion to combine the OSS and SSO into a single entity—the Strategic Conflict Actuation Group, SCAG. No response yet.

In his attempt to filter old memories and visages and delete Illuminé membership, the doctor had unwittingly swapped memories of the two. The operation was intended to maintain their operational knowledge, not scramble their brains.

Unknown to the president, the two CIA leaders had been rescued from the Langley rubble and taken to Doctor Rorschach, their doctor of record. It wasn't clear to him if his experiments with them were fully successful. He attached them once again to his computer.

"That you stare continuously at the ceiling perhaps may bother you."

The catatonic patients indicated no response.

They barely breathed.

"Please. Do not allow my white lab coat, and the instruments, and the computer attached to your crania—pardon me, craniums—to cause you anguish. I assure you, I am the preeminent doctor of memories in the entire world."

The patients remained oblivious.

"And the two of you are safely fastened to the twin operating tables. You, DCI, performed as Director of Central Intelligence. And you ..." He surveyed his other patient. "... DDCI, the deputy. Oh, I'm being inconsiderate. Are you comfortable?"

No response.

"About your membership in the Illuminé secret organization—"

The locked doors burst open as if struck by a tank.

"I have to stop this!" said a stocky man who stomped the twenty feet to the other three.

"Who—"

Guards flew into the room as if shot out of a cannon. Before they could hustle the intruder away, he threw an electrical breaker in the midst of a mental swap.

The guards pulled the doctor away from his patients, in spite of his vociferous protests in Swiss-German.

With Rorschach absent, the patients exhibited confusion as to who each was, but found their Illuminé memories restored.

In quick order, they agreed to pretend to be each other.

Later, and under Jack Sommers orders, they'd be taken to a safe house, where, unknown to him, they initiated an operation to wipe out the Crayle team.

CHAPTER 26

Spring arrived and pleasant weather ensued. The chilly, negative temperature nights would transition over the next months to the upwards of 47-degree Celsius heat that was no stranger to the deserts of the Northern Territories of Australia. It was comparable to the skin-burning 117-degree Fahrenheit temperatures of southern Nevada and Arizona.

The Red Centre was so named for the reddish color of the soil. Flights arriving at the Ayers Rock Airport gave away the extent of the geological anomaly to all who trekked here for the wondrous sights, the center of which was the Ulurú—the giant dome.

The dome was more like a 2.2 mile long, 1,000 foot high reddish loaf of bread made of the arkose sandstone that had plummeted from the heavens and stuck deeply into the soft terrain. Whenever the French visited, it was pointed out that Ulurú was approximately 24 meters—78 feet—higher than the Eiffel Tower.

The aboriginals of the country held their icon to high religious significance. The leaders had just arrived as a prelude to a gathering of them all. All tribes. They represented the remaining fifty of the original 700 languages that existed before the Europeans arrived. Things needed desperately to change. A microphone had been supplied to ensure that no attendee could later say they didn't hear.

The meeting held in the Cultural Centre near the rock contained only ten attendees. The leader spoke.

"Welcome to you all. I will speak in English for those of you from tribes that no longer require your children to learn the ancient tongues. Once we succeed on our quest, the original lands of the Indigenous will no longer be in dispute. We will ask the non-indigenous, kindly and peacefully, to exit our sacred lands. That includes the miners who have burrowed into the lands, lands created by our hallowed ancestors during the *Tjukurpa* period, with sacrilegious fervor. With that brief opening, I would like to introduce you to one of our most profound acolytes. She is called Kianna and, as you gentlemen will surely note, a beautiful rendition of our kind." He turned to a woman who wore a floor-length, tight-fitting, purple dress that precisely fit her perfect figure. She stood, gave a brief bow, and stepped to the microphone.

"*Palya!* Hello in my Anangu tribal language. I realize there are several of the remaining dialects represented here. Full disclosure, I was actually born in Tasmania to my aboriginal parents, grew up there, and attended university. As you can see, my English is quite passable as a result. I will see to any translations so that all can understand, because this necessity before us is not just about the Anangu, on whose land sits the great red rock. It is about us all."

• • •

The rock appeared as always, its stunning, god-like beauty transcending the scrub-ridden, flat red outback. The aboriginals approached their sacred stone. Their ritual, as it had since the beginning, honored the sacrosanct Ulurú as the Sun descended, and the rock's daytime hue transformed into something mystical and magical.

Whether the natives actually saw the bright flash would be unknown at this time. Nuclear devices seldom provided time to appreciate their splendor.

The flash before the two men immediately blew Ulurú into its component dust particles originally deposited in an upheaval 50,000,000 years before.

Having delivered their final respects, the natives vaporized.

Their blood, too, vaporized to blend with the now-red atmosphere throughout the surrounding area.

The two men were pleased. The larger one assessed.

"Your 75-inch, ultra-HD screen portrays the realization of your ultimate goals. The attendant high-end sound system caused me to feel the devastation. Nicely done. You shall be rewarded." He reached over.

The other one clinked glasses. "At this distance, we are safe from the total destruction of an icon."

"The destruction …"

"If I may correct you, our reward shall reach fruition only when we move to reality from the exquisite simulation we have just witnessed."

"Nothing really. Not a challenge given my skills."

"We must make it real before someone interferes with our great dream."

The other raised his glass. "To the destruction of the rock … and the subsequent civil war!"

They clinked once more.

"To the destruction of Australia!"

CHAPTER 27

Australian mining magnate Hamilton Farrell's adjutant and soothsayer, Kianna Tarni, rubbed back and forth once again. Except for the opinions of those Australians who might be bigots or full-on racists regarding aboriginals, she was quite beautiful. Just 5'7", the top of her head matched up with his lips as if he were meant to kiss her on the forehead, as one would a daughter. Her ringlet black curls topped off the exotic image.

That the man she faced was slightly round about the waist belied his years ago experience in the Aussie Rules Football league. Tough as nails, they said. They were right. Except they were unaware of the dramatic character change he would undergo later in life. His life-changing experience had been bad news for those who found his bad side; not a difficult task at all.

"Tell me again," she beckoned.

"I've told my story to you several times now, my Kianna, each under the same conditions. Besides, reclining in this chair, naked, I'm getting a chill. Move so I may alight and don my togs."

She remained lying fully clothed, her back against his chest, her legs dangling between his to the floor. "Just once more. As in the past, I promise not to interrupt."

She slid slowly down his body.

"Well, if you insist. One would think that you are writing a book."

"Or collecting intelligence."

He glanced down.

"Your intelligence, Ham, of course." She'd just taken an unnecessary risk with her word selection. A deadly risk. Her heart skipped a beat.

"That you acknowledge my intellect endears me to you. You know that."

She began on him.

"I commenced into existence with a very planned pregnancy. My father hailed from a small town between east coastal Newcastle and the Australian wine country, Hunter Valley. Morpeth is its name. Not too far north of Sydney. My mother was a product of Akaroa, South Island, New Zealand. With its French heritage. Both of long-ago nobility. Both descendants of former convicts."

She stopped for just a second. "An Aussie and a Kiwi. Interesting. And what did they want for you?"

"Mother wanted me to be a solicitor. A lawyer. She'd gotten hooked on the Perry Mason series about an incredible defense attorney. Hence the name she gave me. After the district attorney, Hamilton Burger."

"And your father?"

"He wanted me to be a miner like himself. He won."

His story stopped abruptly. He entered into a coughing spasm, for just a few seconds. He regained his composure in short order.

"Do you realize that when you do that, you cast my tensions to the winds."

She continued unabated. She hoped that this time would lead to a final turn of the tumbler—the one that unlocked the heretofore impregnable safe that was his mind. His physical response to her efforts caused gaps in his speech, plus a panting sound.

"I'm going to blow up … blow up … ahhh!" He gasped an aboriginal vulgarity.

CHAPTER 28

The Australian showered, then donned his outback uniform of khaki shorts and a matching Eisenhower jacket over a light tan shirt. As he finished with his school tie, he caught a glimpse of a now fully naked, exceptionally beautiful Kianna in the mirror.

"My dear, that was exceptional. We must do this again when I return."

"Return. From where?" Her tone was playful, but her intent intense.

"Top Secret, my dear. But I shall be returning in just a few days, hopefully to remain forever. I'll be having a quite serious conversation with you. Dwell on that, as you wish."

Before she could respond in an attempt to coax detail from his lips, the Australian mineral magnate's chief goon entered.

A modest-under-the-circumstances Kianna pulled up the bed sheet to cover her torso. The goon paid no attention.

"Ah, there you are, Auger. We must have a moment to discuss your orders during my absence. You will, of course, see to the well-being of my adjutant, Ms. Tarni. The rest we shall discuss in private."

He'd dressed before summoning Auger, the well-built former Rugby and Aussie Rules Football player who ran the non-mining and security aspects of the Farrell operations. The man wasn't treated to the sexual scene he'd have witnessed otherwise.

Farrell glanced over at the sheet-wrapped, youngish woman as she exited the chamber to the bathroom. "Take a seat, Auger."

"Thank you, Mr. Farrell." He sat.

"As you are aware, we have stolen from our Royal Navy the top secrets for acquiring and utilizing sounds. Originally received from the Americans, we have used our new system derived from those stolen software programs to find gold, uranium, and diamonds, each in their own mine, but in proximity to one another. The trio shall make us all excessively wealthy. I've even coined the term G-U-D, pronounced as in the word, GOOD."

Auger smiled. "Yes, sir. GUD became the name of your company. I happened to realize that the name is DUG spelled backwards. As in mining."

"I am suitably impressed. The programs have given us accuracy to 3 mm of the locations of these precious items. We have added a mapping capability to show the correct size and shape and depth of each deposit."

"Everyone in Australia is impressed with your continued successes, Sir."

The Aussie nodded. "And well beyond. Enough bowing and scraping, Auger. In preparation for my trip, you will need to take the uranium cake, wrap it in those blankets next to the wall, and spirit it to its destination hidden in our massive coal deliveries to China."

"I find it hard to believe that blankets of any sort can prevent radioactive rays from escaping. Because of the bulk of the shipments, there is no way the uranium will be detected. I believe I have the proper destination documents, unless there have been changes."

"Nothing has changed. It's Shanghai. Our ship's captain will be met by the Chinese Empress Ling's representative when the pilot boat pulls alongside. They will load from the ship to their trucks immediately after docking. There will only be a pass-by of the port officials. They are all on the pad."

"On the pad?"

"It's an Americanism, Auger. On the pad, on the take. They mean the same thing: corrupt. The uranium will be extracted from the load on the way to its destination. Then, the precious material will be delivered to the bomb factory. I expect to meet it there after my tète-a-tète with the Empress in Hong Kong. Expect me back within the week."

"Yes, Sir."

"Oh, and Auger. As I have said before, see to Miss Tarni's security while I am away. If anyone ventures near, you know what to do. You've done it before. Lastly. I know she's quite attractive. Don't be tempted. Your life depends on it."

"I believe I understand your relationship, Sir. Please feel you can trust me."

"Right. That will be all, Auger. I'll see you when I return."

Auger left the room. Farrell always wondered why someone in that man's position always asked for trust. The statement always begat the question: Is there some reason I should not trust you?

CHAPTER 29

The deceased Chin Yao-wu's former disciple known as Yellow Daughter led a quite regal appearing Empress Ling An-yee into the Hong Palace's visitor's room. There, she would meet for the first time the anxious Australian, Hamilton Farrell.

A Dassault Falcon jet with an Australian flag painted on its side landed in the early afternoon. The old Kai Tak Airport in Hong Kong Harbour had been turned into a cruise terminal, the new airport digs now at Chep Lap Kok Airport. It resided on a tiny eponymous island, which sat a stone's throw away on the north side of the much larger Hong Kong neighbor, Lantau Island.

The road to the city of Hong Kong from Lantau was circuitous at best. It appeared from the air as a backward **C** shape, taking one east to Kowloon city on the mainland, then around through the harbor tunnel to its destination. It provided serious sightseeing opportunities for tourists and long delays for those who had business in one of the globe's premier cities.

A limousine in royal purple deposited Hamilton Farrell and his extensive luggage at the Victoria Peak palace of Empress Ling. He'd left his number one lieutenant, Kianna, back at the mining sites to oversee operations, with every confidence she would accomplish the task. And see to his interests. Still, his nerves felt anything but calm.

The VIP visitor's ingress could not be as straightforward as he would like. Whoever visited the empress represented prime fodder for gossip. Especially for the ever present media.

It had all been arranged. The Australian donned a disguise and joined a party that had sought a royal audience. Since the governance of China had just changed drastically from communist to imperialist, the emissaries wished to pursue complete sovereignty versus their long-standing 'autonomous region' status under the communists.

Inside the Hong Kong palace's royal chambers, Ling readied for her day. On top, a meet with the aforementioned Muslim delegation from Xinjiang in China's far west. The meeting lasted thirty minutes and produced a firm *I'll consider your request*, after which, all departed save one. The remaining individual removed 'her' burka to reveal a man—one Hamilton Farrell. As much as he'd wanted to jump in with his valuable insights, he spoke not one word during the confab. A men only affair, he chose not to give himself away as other than female.

"Welcome, Mr. Farrell. I've been made aware of your desires. You are here to purchase mini-nukes to be manufactured from uranium your company in Australia has mined and sent, hidden in a huge coal shipment, to my country. Yellow Daughter indicates the shipment was received in Shanghai, removed and verified elsewhere. I believe you have delivered as payment one bag of perfect, single-carat diamonds you purchased via an intermediary from Mr. Lenny Lipschitz in Amsterdam—with help from Swiss bankers. Very special Swiss bankers."

"You are well informed. I wish to thank you for your hospitality, Empress, but I really must collect my goods—the four mini-nuclear devices—and be on my way. I would love to stay and enjoy your company and this wondrous city, but am regrettably under a severe time constraint. Please forgive my rudeness."

"You are forgiven. There will be no beheadings today."

Farrell blanched at the thought.

“Consider that Imperial humor, Mr. Farrell. I understand time constraints. I have them myself. It is a pity. I have several women who would see to your relaxation. The Japanese are not the only ones who provide that manner of steam bath. You could leave truly relaxed.”

“Perhaps when I become leader of my country, I shall return for such favors. But not now.”

“Very well. Yellow,” she called out.

Her number two entered. She produced the requisite bow to each of them and awaited her orders.

“See that the implements are suitably packed such that my guest may spirit them back to his country for deployment.” She turned back to her new client. “You will find that Yellow is nothing if not efficient. I am certain you sent your private jet to be refueled as soon as you landed, so, without further ado, I bid you adieu.”

Ling waved her hand from him toward Yellow Daughter, who politely bowed once again.

The Australian turned and exited past the two massive eunuchs left over from the Chin period. They guarded the doorway.

When Yellow returned, she crossed the Grand Hall to a window where Ling stood to watch her new client enter the limo and drive off.

“Will he be back?”

“You never know. But we are running out of purchasers for our goods. We’ve deployed our wares to Europe, the Middle East, Asia, and now Australia. Other than the two frozen continents, that leaves only Africa … and America untouched. So far. Consider them, Yellow, in your planning. And consider that operating my palace with all the guards, chefs, and caretakers is expensive. Economic times for China are not good. The previous custodians, the Communists, decided to poke the sleeping tiger, America, in the eye and their economic retaliation was swift and brutal.”

Yellow began a song. “There must be some kind of way out of here …”

"... said the joker to the thief. Hmmm. *All Along The Watchtower.* Bob Dylan. Jimi Hendrix with the cover." Ling produced a meager smile. "I miss him."

"The joker or the thief?"

"Magus."

"He's married. Wife Hekka is with child. Best to forget him."

"Best, but not easy."

Dismissed, Yellow headed to the castle library to begin consideration of new markets for the miniature nuclear devices.

Ling transited to her own watchtower, there to survey her realm. Hong Kong, Kowloon, and all of China beyond.

CHAPTER 30

Micmac and Phoebe drove the short distance from Yorktown, Virginia, to Norfolk and transited the *Chesapeake Bay Bridge–Tunnel* system north to the Virginia southern portion of the Maryland peninsula. They imagined boats passing overhead while in the tunnel, and then viewed them actually doing so from the bridge. Watching the Chesapeake Bay empty its waters into the Atlantic Ocean provided serene pleasure for Phoebe.

"Keep your eyes glued on the dash GPS. I want to make all the correct turns to stay on schedule."

"Aye, aye, Sir."

A smile and a nod. "Did you enjoy the pub?"

"I did. Did you see the sign inside … over the front window?"

"THE ANCIENT MARINER INN. Made me feel born again."

"As in Jason Bourne?"

"Could he swim?"

"Apparently."

"I think I'll leave being a spy to the real one. To Magus."

Bored at watching their vehicle's symbol eeking along, Phoebe glanced up from their ride's video display.

"It's beautiful, Mick. But the sign ahead says Highway 13. Can you find an alternate route?"

"Not and make our timeline."

"I vote that we reject the notion of timelines after this."

"We'll lunch in the quaint fishing village called Annapolis."

"Which happens to contain the Naval Academy *which* you attended."

"Coincidence. After, we'll hit Quantico so you can kiss the sainted Fibbee earth, and hand over a copy of Magus' new spy thriller, like you told him you would."

"I've thought about that. If I show up at Quantico, my old FBI boss in D.C. will be alerted. He didn't want to give me up to Project Crayle in the first place."

"Yeah. But Magus jumping in to save the current president's hind end up there in the Bering Sea caused a major marker."

"It wasn't my fault. I'd been detailed to exfil an NSA operative, now our president. I got stuck in Nome, Alaska. The CIA provided Magus for the exfil. Hence, the indelible marker. That said, I'm going to skip Quantico and D.C. as well."

"What about Magus' novel? You were going to … wait! You said that in order to get a copy to read before anyone else."

"Hekka, Alona, and I have formed a new organization. Sneaky R Us. Catchy, huh?"

"Hmmm. Well, our kid is going to be raised straight up. No sneaky for him. SEAL-like."

"Him?"

• • •

The pair stopped off for lunch at Don's Seafood and Chicken House and Pub for lunch. The cartoon seagull replete with pirate's hat and eye patch set the mood for the former sailor. They chose

Crab Cakes for appetizers and *Sweet Baby Ray BBQ Ribs* for an entrée from the menu, chowed down, then continued toward their midway destination. Feeling good.

After passing through numerous stands of thin trees, Micmac crossed a bridge over the Chesapeake Bay northward aspect. He followed his nose rather than the GPS to downtown Annapolis. As he stopped in front of his favorite little restaurant, he nodded Phoebe's attention to the picture-perfect boat harbor to their left.

Once she'd alighted, he set off to a nearby parking garage and returned in fifteen minutes. With Phoebe nowhere in sight, he smiled, then headed to the nearby Starbucks. He'd find her inside.

A sign outside the Starbucks specialty coffee shop brought a second smile. *Welcome to your Military Family Store.*

They stepped inside.

• • •

After a quick caramel latte, a straight coffee, and a large dose of salt air, the pair circumvented the Washington, D.C. quagmire and headed south. Toward Richmond, Virginia. Toward the airport and the flight home.

CHAPTER 31

With Alona having commandeered the car keys, Lenny whined, then acquiesced into a responsible attitude as he accepted his default role as navigator. When she stopped to fill the car with gas, Lenny went inside the 7/11 style establishment and made a purchase he deemed a necessity relative to his new job description.

He scanned the Virginia page of the AAA Easy Reading Road Atlas he'd just purchased for the way forward. With several intersections coming up, Alona prodded him.

"I need a direction, sport. What you got?"

"There's a place out west from here called Lynchburg."

"You make one of your jokes and I'd be betting on the lynch part."

"Okay. No Lynchburg. Oh, right near here. The original burg, as they say, for the colonists. Jamestown." He stopped. "Hey, there go Magus and Hekka. Wonder why they're turning off there. Let's follow 'em."

"Our orders are to split off, two-by-two, my dear. We're leaving them be."

"We could have their backs—just in case."

"The Crayles are quite lethal. They don't need us backing them up. If that .40 caliber of his and Bowie of hers had notches for all the BG's they've taken down, you wouldn't be able to see the weapons for the notches."

"Okay. Jamestown. Make a left."

"Where?"

"Back there."

• • •

Fifteen minutes later, they arrived at the colonial remnants of Jamestown.

"The river right there is the James. Must've named the town after it."

"Why don't you come up with a few names for our child, rather than continue with your Improbable History."

"Like Peabody the dog? On Rocky and Bullwinkle?"

She ignored him. It was a well developed skill.

It didn't work. "I'd still like to know why Magus and Hekka turned off at a military base."

"Because you're nosy."

"I'm a P.I. Nosy is an asset. What I am."

"I'll let that one slide."

"Whine."

• • •

Once at the monument to the Jamestown ruins, things didn't go well. Lenny demanded a photo op. A reluctant Alona agreed.

"Stand in front of that fence made of sharpened poles."

"One better." Lenny climbed to the top. "Shoot me up here."

Alona pushed the wrong thoughts aside. "Hey! The sign says, DON'T CLIMB ON FENCE."

"Who's gonna know?"

No sooner did he mount the meticulously restored wooden rampart, than it started to tilt. Then, more. Finally, following a loud crack, his section collapsed. With the sections bonded together for added strength, they followed suit in short order. Like dominoes.

Miraculously unhurt, Lenny scrambled up from the ground, ran to his disbelieving wife, and grabbed her hand.

Onlookers stood transfixed as if mimicking the various historic statues in the park.

"*Earthquake!*" Lenny yelled. He pulled Alona with him at a run.

Having witnessed the devastation, the others, too, began to run for their vehicles.

As Alona sped them from the man-made catastrophe, Lenny couldn't contain himself. "Great save, huh?"

"I told you, DON'T CLIMB ON FENCE."

"*Whine!*"

CHAPTER 32

Magus & Hekka headed out as tensions and fears generated by the southeast battles wound down.

With Hekka in the passenger seat, Magus Crayle drove his rental SUV back up the Highway 64 but didn't take the turnoff to the left for their hotel. This time, he took the clearly marked Exit 238 off ramp to Highway 143 East.

Hekka had seen the signs. "Why are we heading for Camp Peary? What's there?"

"I've got to drop something off. My first novel."

"You spent our child's college money on editing and publishing *your* book?"

"Don't forget our share of the millions from the diamonds."

"And don't you forget that Heidi and Astrid still need to set up access to said millions."

A vision of him working at McDonalds for their kid's tuition flashed through Crayle's mind.

"You haven't even shown it to me. What title did you choose?"

"Remember Lalumière and the diamonds he received as bribes? From selling water priorities in the Middle East? I chose, as my title, *The Water Diamonds*."

"Before you explain, I get it. The diamonds from the water."

"Well done, my fellow spy."

"It makes me think of our lake."

"The Water Diamonds?"

"The afternoon sparkle from the setting sun. Hundreds of water diamonds."

"My gift to you."

She glanced at her ring finger. "I'm happy with this one."

The off ramp terminated at a tree-isolated, asphalt pad. On the far side, razor wire topped fences and a guarded entry point. Crayle avoided any potential personal inspection, search, and surveillance one accepted by physically entering the Army base by swinging the SUV to a stop, and jumping out, hands held high.

A young guard, his superior off taking a leak in the forest, flew out of his guard shack, weapon in hand. Unsure of the circumstance, he fell back on his training. "Drop your weapon!"

Crayle waved the book he held aloft in his left hand. "This new international spy thriller is my only weapon, soldier. Your commandant is expecting it. It's her personal, inscribed copy. To be placed in the library at The Farm."

The guard winced. It seemed he was aware of the CIA's newby training facility on the base grounds.

"Please take it so we can leave."

The guard gestured with his M-4. "Place it on the ground."

Crayle complied, saluted, re-entered the vehicle and departed the way he'd come, leaving a half past dumbstruck young soldier to ponder his fate.

Engrossed with phone updates from the MacKays and Lipshitzes, Hekka asked the operative question. "Not a problem, was it? Where to now?"

"Tell you what. Let's drive to the Blue Ridge Mountains. The parkway provides fabulous views, not just of the mountains, but the verdant valleys to either side. And the famous Shenandoah River. Where peace and tranquility abound."

Her answer was a smile and three little words he never tired of hearing. "I love you, Mr. Crayle."

• • •

The drive west was uneventful. Lines of trees down both sides of the 64 no doubt planted to contain traffic noise also precluded views of the intervening landscape. Just over two-and-a-half hours, with stops for potty breaks, they reached one of several Blue Ridge Mountains visitor centers.

Crayle picked up a guide to the area and perused it while Hekka checked out the gift shop. "We should buy some things for the others. Virginia has so much beauty, I believe they'll all want to come back. So will I, along with our new baby, and with an absolute lack of bullets flying. That's non-negotiable."

"We'll head down a ways. There's a spot called Big Spy Mountain Overlook at 3,200 feet where we can overlook the Shenandoah River. Sounds as if it was made just for us. It is supposed to be quite beautiful. We can follow the Blue Ridge Parkway, and then head back to the Richmond airport via Charlottesville, or south on the same road to Roanoke. Any preference?"

"What's the delta?" she said from the checkout counter.

He grinned. "You sound like Micmac. The delta is that the northern route is faster, the southern has more sights."

"Let's go south. I want to be able to tell our little girl about it someday, and then bring her here."

He nodded.

"Ouch!" Hekka felt her tummy. "That was your son."

"I thought we were having a girl. Genders don't change out of convenience."

"Now you tell me."

Crayle's phone rang. "Sorry," he said to the proprietor. "I'll take it outside."

The fresh breeze of the hills brought Crayle wide awake. But not as much as the voice on the other end.

"Hello, Magus. Hope you are okay down there in the Blue Ridge. I've been read in on your recent traumatic episodes, the sort that your Mr. Lipschitz seems to attract."

"I'm glad you know about it, Mr. President. I'd like not to relive the recent past, not even in dialog."

"That you're in one piece is important to me as a friend, but also since you once saved my sorry butt off the coast of Alaska. When I was NSA. And, I admit, because I have a selfish interest. Namely, that you did promise to restructure the CIA post apocalypse with that nuclear device Chin's daughters detonated over the HQ."

"We lost the top two floors at Langley. Only because the bomb delivered by airburst underperformed. Could've been the whole schlemiel."

"Operational status?"

"The computers are below ground and hardened. They're okay. The old wired comms gear is pretty much toast, but the uber-secure Wi-Fi is already up and running. Unfortunately, the protective shell was breached and broken with the loss of six and seven."

"So anyone nearby can listen in?"

"It's still encrypted, so it would take a China or Russia to even have a prayer."

"Speaking of prayers, what's the status of our Iranian friends?"

"We got a hot tip that their top nuke guy—Mohammed something or other—went up with the recent detonation in China. The one that took out Chin and the French leaders."

"That one released radiation, unlike the others in this string of explosions. Right?"

"Yes, Sir. You're right about that. And I did make that promise to you. And I greatly appreciate your confidence in me to that end. But, and I'm not flexible on this, Hekka and I need time off until the baby is born. Actually, let's shoot for a couple of weeks afterwards."

"When is she due?"

"Within four weeks, Sir."

"Whew. That's tough on this end. I might apply pressure by saying that it is also tough on your country, but I won't do that. I hope in the interim that the world will not continue on its current course, i.e., falling apart." President Stones paused a second. "Look, I get where you are on this. I wish you the best of luck. Any idea where you can go in order to be outside the target zone for all these fanatics and their armies?"

"I do. I'll share it with you because I need your help. But no-one can know. Above Top Secret. Sensitive Information. Agreed?"

"Agreed. But, not even Jack Sommers?"

"Not even Jack."

"Like I said. This is a tough one, but you've more than earned it. Take care, and let me know if you need any help—also in my selfish interest—and I'll be there for you. And Hekka. As you surely recall, I'm a specialist at help with governments. I do that one quite well."

"Yes, Sir. And thank you. Really."

"Okay, Magus. President out."

He returned inside the visitor center where Hekka stood patiently, shopping bags in hand. "Who was that?"

"Wrong number. I told them that we were on the National Do Not Call Registry. They didn't want to listen."

"Brother. Some people."

"Yeah."

• • •

The Crayles left the visitor center with T-shirts, fridge magnets, shot glasses, for the adults, and a onesy for each of the babies.

The trip along the Blue Ridge Parkway was all it was touted to be, and more. A few hours later, they headed back toward their airport rendezvous at the state capitol, Richmond. The trip had morphed into something neither they nor their team members could have imagined. Not even in a severe nightmare. Not to dwell on, though. It would get a lot worse.

CHAPTER 33

Back home and back to work, Micmac and his crew of SEAL Team Six, retired, volunteers continued to remediate the recent severe damage to Magus and Hekka Crayle's cabin in the Fawnskin neighborhood of Southern California's Big Bear Valley.

Lenny, who'd just dragged the team through a death-defying romp through the American southeast stood by, but couldn't keep quiet. "There must be a law about exploding a tree onto someone's home."

Micmac responded as he pulled lengths of damaged wood from the rubble. "Don't know. But I'll bet there is insurance. For the Crayles, I mean."

"When an eighty-foot tree crashes down on your cabin, you can expect to write it off."

"It seems that the rules for that sort of thing are constantly changing. Maybe your attorney wife can help with that one."

"And the men's work continues apace."

"How'd you do that?"

"What'd I do?"

"Get the girls to go shopping."

"Oh, that. One: them being about nine months along, they wouldn't be able to help rebuild a cabin. Two: their hormones might get in the way. Three: shopping will relieve their tension."

Micmac pursed his lips. He took a moment to give thumbs up to his crew of SEAL Team Six retirees as their leader indicated with a hand signal that they were at a temporary stopping point, but prepared to continue on until dusk.

He turned back to the P.I. "After our battles in the southeast—with that army of hair-challenged fanatics—a high spending, low testosterone diet is just the thing."

"Yeah. Ya know, when I first heard that word, hormone, I thought they said whore moan."

Micmac decided to humor the questionable humorist. He fed him the next line. "And what did you say?"

"Well, yeah!" Lenny laughed.

Micmac shook his head. SOP. "Hey, toss me that nail gun."

Lenny picked up the referenced item and hefted it over. "You're great at fixing stuff. So, before Jack roped me into all of this, how'd you get Mag's Cobra back together after his big accident in Malibu totaled it? You, know, the crash that Sylvain Lalumière's crew caused."

"The wannabe King of France? He either went up with that nuke in Monte Carlo or has gone way off the grid. I haven't heard anything from Mr. Jack Sommers about any of that. You?"

"Not a word. Jack's up to his eyeballs trying to run what's left of the CIA for President Stones. Maybe you could help rebuild their HQ at Langley after we're done here. By the way. Where are Magus and Hekka?"

"They're probably staying away from you after this recent gig."

"Okay, okay. Lay off, sailor. My bad."

Micmac hefted the end of a replacement joist. "You want to help me with this?"

"No. But thanks for asking. I gotta run. Stuff to do around the house."

"You haven't done anything here."

"Oh, that was painful."

"Nothing like your jokes."

"I should start charging."

"Yes. And start offering discount coupons. You'll make a fortune."

The two men, as different as humanly possible, shared a chuckle. Lenny cut his short.

"Remember when Jack brought Magus here from the Quarry hospital in a coma? And the Lalumière bunch assaulted the place?"

"Seems the bad guys always have unofficial armies. Too bad they picked on the wrong crew, us, to attack."

"We're just that good. Now if you could just get your wife to adjust her attitude toward me. And Hekka. I was being my usual humorous self on the plane ride home, and she flashed the sunlight from the window in my eyes. With that ten-inch Bowie knife of hers. At least, Alona loves me."

Their heads snapped around to a yell from the roadway on the other side of the cabin.

"*Lenny! Help me!*"

Micmac recognized the voice. "There's Alona now."

"She'll be fine.

Micmac started to counter.

"No, no," Lenny held up his hands. "Trust me. She'll be fine."

Then, a crash of packages fumbled to the ground. Alona came around the back of the cabin apace. "Where *is* that little twerp?"

CHAPTER 34

Magus and Hekka Crayle sat in the cabin of the Dassault Falcon 7X. They'd experienced infrequent bouts of turbulence over the ocean, but the pilot kept the aircraft at high enough altitude to mitigate the effects. The passengers received the usual royal treatment not usually reserved for those who did the CIA's bidding.

"I related this to you early in our flight. I'd like to recount our history together. Later, if you don't object. Let me know if in the hours passed I've forgotten something, or misspoken. Okay."

She smiled. "You don't forget important things. But, go ahead."

"When we finished with Lenny's debacle, and you and I went on our way from Williamsburg, I cobbled a deal with President Stones. You and I get an unabated two week vacation or post partum, whichever came first."

"We already know whoever came first."

"That is Lenny humor. Not allowed."

"No, that's my humor."

"I'm sorry."

"You should be."

"That your jokes aren't any better than his."

Hekka's Bowie lay on a nearby table. She reached for it.

"Okay, all right. I shall cease and desist from comparing your jokes with the P.I.'s Fair enough?"

"It's a deal. Now. I want to hear from your strategic planner self. Magus Crayle two of three. Every detail. Where will the itinerary you picked take us?"

He smiled at her. The way lovers do during the first months. Those were past for the couple. They chose to relive that essence repeatedly. "We'll land in Auckland. Say goodbye to Jack's wife—our Brazilian pilot, Flori—and then we'll board the Emerald Princess cruise liner."

"Emerald. I like that. I'm a veritable Serrano Indian Princess, so it fits. And Auckland? New Zealand? That's perfect. I can hook up with the native Maori there. Offering you up for one of their ritual sacrifices would be a sure in for me."

"While I agreed during our wedding ceremony to make any sacrifices necessary, that one hadn't occurred to me."

"Since our child is going to need a dad, I think I'll pass on the sacrifice." She pinched her nose. "Recalculating."

The two shared a good laugh, a sure sign of their transition from stressed to tension free.

• • •

When their flight arrived in Auckland, New Zealand, the Crayles collected their luggage and caught a cab to the pier. They flashed their black Elite Captains Circle passes at check-in, and were quickly escorted aboard the Emerald Princess. Like all ships of that cruise line, a stylized, dark blue graphic portraying a sea witch adorned each side of the ship's bow.

They'd cruised before. The distinguished liner, Queen Mary 2, had been somewhat larger, and with more pomp and circumstance than the more casual Emerald. And the latter of the two was far less likely to have had a mini-nuke spirited aboard.

The common factors between the two carriers were that both had pools, a grand theater, 24/7 food and beverage venues, and a private space, their cabin, to find peace and solitude, and time together. Just them.

They visited Tauranga for a native Maori village and war dance. Hekka felt an unusual oneness with the Maori people. Almost magical. She connected before a single word had been spoken.

The cruise ship moved on to Gisborne and a steam train ride. Then, to the capitol of New Zealand, Wellington, with its *sine qua non* relationship to the several Lord of the Rings productions that included a hillside filming site and the production studio.

The more they cruised and saw, the more relaxed they became. They wondered if that were true of the other passengers. All except those who'd brought children. But the kids' frenetic behaviors, especially around and in the pool, brought smiles. They would bring their own kids someday on such a fun-packed and educational journey.

The Emerald Princess continued on to the eastern shoreline of New Zealand's South Island to a little town on a little cove called Akaroa. Interestingly, it had originated as a French rather than British colony. Still, it sported street names in French such as *Rue Jolie*. Or, Pretty Street.

Further south on the west side of the large island, they ported at Dunedin, a Scottish name. The pair spent the full day on a train ride into the interior. To a place called Taieri Gorge. The weather in the interior reminded them that the cooling trend of Fall at their home had morphed into the warming trend of the Spring in the Down Under. Warm. Slightly humid.

"Magus, this is so beautiful. In fact, the two large islands of New Zealand exhibit beauty after beauty. It's non-stop."

"The Kiwis—that's what they're called—have plenty for which to be thankful."

"For which?"

"I'm working on my English language skills. I'm a writer now, you know."

"You should work the sights and people from this trip into your future stories."

"Now there's a novel idea."

"Groan … no … whine!"

"When we return, I'm notifying the Centers for Disease Control. Lenny and his humor are contagious. It could turn into a pandemic."

They smiled at each other just before they shared a long and sensuous kiss. They were happy. They were at peace. And life was good. They could breathe easy now.

A day later, they arrived on the southwest side of the South Island and sailed the vastness and natural wonder of Doubtful Sound. They spent several hours touring the fjords. Deep gorges and pristine vistas, pure cool air, vertical cliffs, and caves along the water's edge. A village sat quietly on a tiny plot of land that extended from the bottom of one of the cliffs.

They would cruise on to Tasmania during the night, and complete their leisure cruise just a few days later with a morning docking. After eleven days, they'd be ready to check out one of Australia's premier cities.

Hekka stood on their balcony, her husband close by. "I don't want this to end."

"Then I hereby declare that it continue unto eternity. As shall my love for you."

"You have my love forever, Mr. Crayle."

They sealed their emotions with a soft, enduring kiss.

"We still have time for a quickie," Crayle suggested.

"You wouldn't know how to do a quickie. You're a lover. My lover."

"I truly am."

She paused a few seconds to fully consume the words they'd just spoken. She remembered an earlier thought.

"We have some time before we have to track down our next meal. I'm a good listener. Go ahead and unload."

"In varied order, here goes. Since you were part of most of this, let's take turns."

"I'll channel Micmac instead of Lenny. Go."

"A forced crash on Highway One above Malibu."

"An assassination attempt on you at the Big Bear Tack Store."

"An assault at Jack's cabin … with me inside."

"The near terminating fight at Lalumière's château."

"We were captured at the Big Bear Oktoberfest."

"Chased across Mulholland Drive in the Los Angeles mountains out to Malibu."

"We thwarted the destruction of the Disneyland castle south of Munich."

"Our seminal cruise on the Queen Mary 2. No baby aboard, just a nuke."

"Our team prevented the Eiffel Tower from becoming ground zero for the obliteration of Paris … and the French government."

"Okay, stop," she said. "This dialog is ramping my pulse. The details for each traumatic experience flood into my brain."

"Yes. The little guy inside is feeling his first adrenaline rushes."

"His first words are going to be what just happened."

"Deep breath."

"Deep breath."

"Exhale."

"Thanks, Magus. I'm ramping down. We did, of course, leave out details such as myriads of bullets, explosives, knives, and the rest that punctuated the aforementioned scenes."

"Scenes? Did you say scenes? Whoa. I'm seeing books. Lots and lots of books. Novels forever based on experiences."

"Minus the classified stuff."

"I can disguise it. I'll call it fiction. With a disclaimer right there in the front of each book."

"Just remember. I helped loosen the lid."

"You bet. And all this talk has made me hungry."

"Excellent idea. Where?"

CHAPTER 35

After night crossing the Tasman Sea between New Zealand and Tasmania, the Emerald Princess bearing the Crayles docked at Macquarie Point in the Tasman capitol, Hobart.

The pair had doffed their plastic rain ponchos after witnessing water streaks while enjoying a delicious Horizon Court buffet breakfast. Hekka turned to him.

"I know you've arranged our excursions for today, but I just found out about the Cascades Female Factory tour here in the capitol."

"A factory? So much for The Creator."

"The Creator's just fine. Back in the day, women prisoners did needle work and so forth while their children received an education. In the trades, for instance."

"Interesting. Perhaps when we return, we'll swing by."

"When we return, we'll rejoin our ship for departure to Sydney. Four P.M. and we're out of here."

"C'mon. Let's hop on our tour bus before this drizzle turns into a downpour."

The Crayles climbed aboard their clearly-marked bus whereupon he chose seats centered on a window. Better for photographing the Tasman terrain.

Time to read Hekka in, he decided.

"We're headed via the Tasman Highway to a historic site about sixty miles from here. On the Tasman Peninsula. It sounds quite interesting as an early prison considering that Australia was later developed by descendents of the convicts. We should be there in about ninety minutes. So relax. Tilt your seat back. Catch a few winks."

"I'm not interested in winks. Now that we're here, I want to see everything."

As they headed out, they observed the number of old brick buildings in quite good repair. Hobart was clean—no street trash.

"That one, there. The Hog's Breath Café built of beautiful yellowish and reddish bricks. I'm sensing a family-friendly place. We'll have to come back some day. Bring our kids."

"Plural kids. We should get started on that tonight."

She pulled his hand onto her distended abdomen. "Note to spy. We need to have this one first."

"We'll cross that bridge."

"When we come to it."

"Like our lives."

"Someday, we'll create a strategy for our lives. Perhaps another one of your genius strategies."

"I agree. But different this time. No more impromptu nuclear events, etc."

"We've started across the famous arched Tasman Bridge."

"Yes, my dear. At approximately 198 feet at its highest, and about 4500 feet in length, the multi-pylon supported bridge carries 6,700 or so cars per day."

She glanced at him in surprise. "So, while I'm at the lectures, and believe you are sleeping, you're up gathering covert intel. And what's all this approximately and about and or so stuff. As a well-worn spy, you could tell me precisely, couldn't you?"

"The exact numbers are, of course, classified."

"You could tell me, but then you'd have to make love to me."

"You've uncovered my scheme."

"Look back across the bay, Hekka. Our ship is magnificent."

"I'm feeling at peace right now. Thank you for kidnapping me to this wonderful adventure. I'll take this to being shot at, any day."

"You're happy. That's all I need."

• • •

They witnessed the beauty of the passing landscape for a while without words. The Down Under offered beauty and bounty in abundance. It required little in terms of verbal observations. Hekka broke the silence.

"Magus, you love data, don't you?"

"We call it intel. The more you know, the more you glow."

"You're hitting a new high on enigma, dear. If we get close enough to one of your so-called mini-nukes, we'll glow all right."

"But that's a good thing. Think how easy it will be to locate our child in the dark."

"What say we move on with our conversation."

"Agreed. But first, those mini-nukes are not mine. They are manufactured, like everything else, somewhere in China. The newly-minted empress, Ling, provides them to megalomaniacs worldwide, without participation from me in the sale or distribution of said devices."

"Boy. Alona the lawyer couldn't have disclaimed it any better."

Hekka decided not to pursue the subject any further. It was her husband's strategy that caused the bombs to be utilized to rearrange the geopolitic. "Look at the forestation of this island. And the crops and the cattle. It gets rural as soon as you leave the city."

Their bus reached a small town.

"I'm feeling the culture."

"Me, too. Check out the Domino's, Subway, and the KFC."

"You're becoming a cynic. I'm placing a limit on your time with Micmac and Lenny."

Past the village, they savored beautiful bay views and several mud flats, one with hundreds of large stones embedded.

At the Port Arthur turnoff, a sign indicated they'd travelled ninety-four kilometers—fifty-eight miles, but the time had passed unnoticed.

Once the bus stopped, and they'd passed through the visitor's entry, they viewed the four-story prison remnants of light-colored brick in the distance. The remaining shell of walls and windows, some barred, gave an impression of what the two thousand prisoners must have experienced. Mother England was a long, long distance away. They'd been exiled. A hard feeling to imagine. The light bricks of the structure gave an airy feel that belied its true nature.

"Let's follow the footpath around to get a better look."

They passed a willow tree so pristine and full, it appeared manufactured. Then trees with acorns large enough to require tools to violate.

They also passed an old church—also of brick—placed there so convicts could seek redemption and forgiveness. Although it was now devoid of any internal accoutrements or stained glass windows, Crayle thought he noticed a genuflecting Catholic. Perhaps offering a prayer. No doubt for prisoners everywhere. He imagined, "Those who have fallen can get back up." He decided to forego a clerical future and just keep his day job.

"That church is more hollowed than hallowed."

"Please accept my request to cease and desist on the Lenny-isms while I enjoy the peace and quiet that surrounds us."

The old prison near the water's edge was next. They took a few minutes to survey the hulk of the 19th Century prison. The moment to reflect on their own better fortunes gave way to the reality of the clock. Time for their bay cruise, Crayle advised.

"We've a boat to catch before we board our bus back to the ship. Let's go."

Hekka strolled alongside her husband to the docking area where they boarded the ferry.

They found a seat with an unobstructed view. He extracted a lifejacket from its hiding place to make sitting more comfortable for Hekka.

Before departing, the ship's sound system provided a recorded safety lecture. Ten minutes later, they cruised the bay.

"I'm not sure one of those life vests will fit me."

"I'll carry you on my back, if necessary."

"Like the scorpion and the frog?"

"Now who's sounding like Lenny?"

She laughed. Just a little.

He was less concerned with channeling Lenny's humor at this point. More so with the white tubes nearby labeled Liferaft Systems Australia—LSA. He wondered if his super-key set from Micmac would open the raft's container, just in case. Regardless, he mentally prepared himself to assure the safety of Hekka and their baby. No matter what.

"Look, Magus. The fisherman over there is holding aloft two 20-plus-inch lobsters. Giant lobsters."

He grinned. "I see. But did he buy them at the store?"

"Question. Who made all of these wonderful travel arrangements? Jack?"

"Not a chance. None of the Langley bunch could know we're going off the grid. Funny you should ask as we pass that building on our left. The Canadian Cottage."

"I don't get it."

"Remember the operative who spirited us by helicopter onto the Queen Mary 2 out there in the Atlantic Ocean? To stop Lalumière and crew from blowing up New York City?"

"I do. A wonderful gentleman on Nova Scotia. I even remember his name. Darryl."

"That's right. A single name. Like a rock star."

"I remember that he waved to us as he rode away on his bicycle. So he made the arrangements for our trip. Thank him when you get the chance. Or … we'll do it in person. Take him out to dinner and drinks. Et cetera."

"Perhaps we'll name our son after him."

"Perhaps he could recommend a nice name for a little girl."

"We need to stop. We're sounding like a Lenny duet."

They laughed a much needed laugh.

"Let's institute a period of silence each time we catch ourselves channeling the P.I. Hmmm?"

"But first, in honor of the Port Arthur prison, name all of the prisons where our arch enemy, Sylvain Lalumière, before his certain death had been incarcerated. It was his own secret society, Illuminé, which harbored him there. With no insignificant assistance from our other deceased friend and psychopath, CIA rogue operative and Illuminé assassin, Pattie Norbrunn."

"Easy. The basement of the Bastille, Marais district, Paris. Château D'If a mile offshore from Marseille. Forte di Exilles in northwest Italy. And last, Sainte Marguerite just offshore of Cannes. France. How'd I do?"

"You get maximum points."

"Is that like getting maximum laid?"

"That sounds like Phoebe."

"Oh? When did Phoebe say that?" She removed her Bowie knife from under her blouse, and gently kissed its sheath.

"I meant that she would say something like that … to Micmac."

She nodded pensively, then returned the Bowie to its hiding place.

The tour of the bay was pleasant. The ferry stopped at the sloped, moderately wooded Point Puer island, where boy prisoners had been housed and educated, and a small, circular, heavily-treed island—home to the Isle Of The Dead Cemetery—about seventy yards across.

Upon returning to shore, the tour bus toted the tourists back to Hobart and the Emerald Princess. The Crayle's utilized the special gangway, such that there would be no inspections that might notice firearms and Bowie knives.

As Hekka had mentioned, the ship organized its Sail Away Party, and set sail at precisely 4 P.M. For Sydney.

CHAPTER 36

It was a noise. A thud.

A motion sensor triggered a bright light. The small room inhabitant's sleep worn eyes sprang open, then descended to slits.

He had no idea where he was. He heard no familiar sounds. Smelled no familiar smells. When his eyes focused, he knew.

His bed was brief. Though it barely accommodated his tall body, it was ultimately comfortable. Yet another Sleep Number mattress.

On a small wooden table, beyond reach through the rusted bars, he saw the CIA dial-a-dose sleep inducement tool.

And the thud. It belonged to a rather small individual lying on the floor. He couldn't yet see her face, but her garment gave her away.

His reaction rendered awestricken an inadequate characterization.

"My precious God!" cried Sylvain Lalumière. "You are back from the dead! At Monte Carlo! The nuclear bomb!"

The woman on the floor emitted a string of expletives.

"You cannot speak that way. You are dressed as a nun."

"Well, this blanking disguise is too blanking long even when I have my blanking stilettos on. Broke one of the blanking spikes."

"Then you must rid yourself of the garments, the habits, that are too long."

"Get rid of my bad habits? Great idea. I'll keep the good ones."

"Is English humor the fault of the language, or of the people?" He performed an eye roll. "Forget what I just said. How did you survive?"

"Simple. At the Grand Prix last May, I stood in front of the Hôtel de Paris between my father—the Prince of Monaco—and the Pope Innocent. Having been selected to present the Grand Prize, I did. To the surprise of everyone, I grabbed the Formula 1 race winner's car, drove out of the casino square, and through the tunnel under the Fairmont hotel. Here's the good part. I knew that Monte Carlo was built on a hump. The ground burst from the mini-nuke bomb I manufactured into the First Place Trophy curved over and down from the square, and then slammed into the Med. It took with it the hotel as I exited the tunnel beneath. The force blew me and that wonderful automobile like a bullet fired into the sea. Good thing I was on the swim team in school. Like I said. Simple."

"You didn't call to let me know what was happening. Or later, to tell me what had transpired."

"It was you who didn't call *me*."

"You had me locked in the old prison on Sainte Marguerite Island. What was I supposed to use …" He waved his arm. "… my cell phone?"

"I get it. Cell. Phone."

"Where are we? Where am I?"

"Not quite as close to the French throne as you were on Sainte Marguerite."

"In that other prison? What you called the last aspect of my grand tour of the incarcerations of the historical Man In The Iron Mask?"

"True it was I, in a stroke of utter brilliance, who concocted you as his modern namesake, Mitim. With my assistance, you played the part. Remember the Rhône River cruise? Remember your song and dance on the Avignon bridge? Right into the hearts of the French people. The prisons were a necessary aspect of your provenance."

"It legitimized me. *Provenance! Merde!*" Lalumière, after lapsing into his native French, returned to English. "You controlled me with those prison cells. Was the original Mitim kept here? Is this the new last one? And, of highest importance, when do I return to France to claim my throne?"

"Hey, boy. Slow down. I didn't just control you by locking you up. I used sex, as well. I think it got you excited when I pretended to be a nun. Most people have to do a lot more than that to get into Hell."

Lalumière's gaze sank to the floor.

"Your second question. No Mitims here but you. Third. I believe this to be the final prison. But, we'll see. Last. I brought some news for you." She tossed him a days-old copy of *Le Monde*.

The Frenchman scooped it from the floor.

"It says that the entire French government that had been hiding in exile was cremated by a nuclear explosion in Xian, China. Along with …" He gasped, "… the new emperor, Chin Yao-wu. You must get me to France, Pattie! She needs me!"

"Easy, cowboy. You know me … and trust me. We'll finish here. Remove a few pains in the ass. Then, and I promise this on my life, we'll go to France, you'll make your entrance to screaming throngs, and you will be crowned formally by the new pope. The old one—it's in the paper on page three—went up with my father. And his latest floozy, that CIA mind doctor, Rikki. And my half-brother. All who stood in my way."

"Yes. The father who created you with a Dutch prostitute. The father who was Prince of Monaco. The father who was the Elder. Leader of the enlightened, the Illuminé."

"That's the one. Good recount, Sylvain. Those new CIA sleep drugs leave no impairment. I'll report the positive result."

"You are rogue. If you contact them, they will find you and kill you. They will kill us both."

She directed him back to the newspaper. "Below the fold."

He flipped it over. "Oh! My son! Jean-Marc! He will marry the Queen of Sweden, it says. No!"

"It's speculation. That's what journalism has become. Can't believe most of it."

"What now?"

"C'mon." She unlocked the cell door.

Hiking up her habit to avoid a replay, she stepped closer. Lalumière, tired and beaten, started up.

Pattie, formerly CIA plant Norbrunn of America's Paris embassy staff and now the Frenchman's wife, shoved him back onto the bed.

As his head contacted the block wall, he cried out. He quickly recovered, and glanced up at her. She'd already rid herself of the nasty habit, now ready to replace it with another.

• • •

The next morning, Sylvain Lalumière peered up from his Sleep Number bed. He checked its display. It was 92. He should have known. Only Pattie could have set his personal number. He squeezed shut his eyes.

Lalumière had awakened to the sounds of a strange animal in the nearby woods.

A devilish wail. He'd been around. The European continent and the Middle East. America. Elsewhere. He'd never heard anything like it. Jungle like, yet ethereal. Scary.

His eyes popped open to reveal yet another set of vertical bars. It served to remind him of the day just passed. And before.

The reality of it all seized him.

"Just another prison! Confined yet again!"

His breathing accelerated until he caught himself just in time. Before hyperventilation.

He removed the cupped hands from his face.

"How did I get here? Where …"

He saw it.

The crystal tube sat at rest on a table not ten feet away. The device Pattie Norbrunn had used to inject the sleep-inducing drugs. 'Dial-A-Dose' she'd called it. Another invention of the CIA's Second Directorate, Science and Technology.

Many times it had deprived him of his senses. Many times he'd awakened in a new place, a new prison. She'd always rationalized his confinements with 'This is one place where the Man-In-The-Iron-Mask was interned. Incommunicado.' Lalumière played his role under the namesake abbreviation, Mitim. He'd heard that name exclaimed in the throes of their sexual encounters. Not his given name, Sylvain. Mitim.

Out of control, he staggered to the table and swept the device to the floor.

Parts of it cracked at the impact.

Not enough.

He stomped and stomped until the smallest fragment was no larger than a pinhead.

It felt very, very good.

Until his breathing stopped. Held.

His mind reverted to the day before. It was an unmentioned side effect of the latest drug.

How did he get here?

How did the device, ever in the possession of his wife, Pattie, get there?

He heard a noise.

Still holding his breath, he looked outside the cell.

A form stepped into the dim light.

Lalumière's jaw nearly came unhinged. Déjà vu all over again.

"You … you … are dead. You … you … were blown to pieces by the bomb. In Monte Carlo. Your father, the Elder … and the Pope …"

His transfixed gaze descended on the apparition to her garments.

"The nun. Again. You disrespect … you …"

"Easy, my French aristocratic homeboy. Let me come inside and fix you up. Know what I mean?"

He remained motionless.

She took a step forward.

Lalumière held up his hands. "Why do I feel that I am experiencing your re-emergence into my life … again? It's like déjà vu."

"All over again? Look. I understand your frustration. From time to time, we covert operatives try out new non-lethal drugs on our own colleagues. It's called an Alpha Test. When we finish with that, we move on outside of our crew to a Beta Test. That would be you."

"You cannot report any results. You are rogue to the CIA."

"They may realize their loss and ask me back at some future date. These results are my bargaining chips. In an obtuse way, I suppose I owe you."

He fairly flew at the bars. "I have destroyed your evil device! Set me free!"

The nun pointed her cross at him, and pressed a circle where the cross pieces met.

Lalumière's arms fell to his sides as he slammed head first into the steel.

Pattie slid the bottom leg from the cross to reveal a razor-sharp, four-inch blade.

"Just in case."

She enacted a cell phone app labeled Holy Crap System.

"Brain scramble … OFF. There. You'll be fine other than a few scrapes and bruises. And the concussion."

The faux nun let herself in with a prop key ring some fake jailer had used to entertain tourists. One he would never again need.

She could see that Lalumière was out cold.

"Oh, my dearest Mitim. Rest well. We have so, so much to do."

• • •

Twenty minutes later, Lalumière regained consciousness.

"Oh, what did you do? No, don't answer. You are a psychopath. Your words."

"*I'm* a psychopath? Who is it that's run all over France claiming to be King Louis the Nineteenth? Claiming to be the modern version of the Man-In-The-Iron-Mask? With his legitimacy dating back to ancestors beheaded during the post-French-Revolution Reign of Terror? And I'm the one who's brainy-brain-brain is split from reality? I'm the psycho?"

"I was named King Louis XIX by a legitimate head of state. The Prince of Monaco."

"Yes. By the man who also headed the ultra-secret society known as Illuminé. Known to his acolytes—love that word—as the Elder. You must remember, he was my father."

"He was still the Prince."

"And how about that pope? The highest religious entity on the planet, perhaps the universe, and he, too, Illuminé. An atheist. I wouldn't be taking your case to court if I were you."

He dropped his face into his hands, moaning both from the physical pain and his ever enduring anguish.

"Not to worry. Sister Magdalena is right here."

"You are condemned to Eternal Hell for what you have done. I want no part of any more of your murderous schemes."

"Oh, but you will. How did I survive an atomic blast in Monte Carlo and live? Easy. God wanted me to survive." Tears welled up. "He needs me."

CHAPTER 37

Pattie had parted from her encounter with Lalumière. He'd take a nap on the Sleep Number bed. The only thing he enjoyed more were his intimate times with her. Small wonder, she thought. She'd learned a lot early on by peeking in on her mother entertaining clients in Amsterdam's finest establishment for that sort of thing.

It was a special day. A sad day. She'd done all she could, but it wasn't enough. It was a bit of a walk to the old relic church, but necessary for what she needed to do. She found it pleasing that she saw no one else either in sight or visible on the prison grounds.

Still dressed in her nun disguise, she genuflected and offered her prayer.

"Forgive me, Father, for I have sinned."

Someone approached from behind. The clop-like footsteps indicated someone of reasonable heft.

A normal person would remain focused on the prayer, and ignore all else. Pattie couldn't. Her line of work forbade such an attitude. Before she could affect a defensive strategy, in case it became necessary, she heard the speaker's words. With a French accent.

"Hello, Pattie. It has been some time for us."

Pattie felt a hand touch her shoulder. "I know the voice. First, your sons. Then, your husband. You're the only one of the triangle jaw household left."

"As you are aware, the Magus Crayle team killed the others."

"You played the role of mother to me. After mine died."

"After she died … at your hands."

"It was necessary."

"As in a CIA operation?"

"Company operatives don't go around murdering prostitutes. And for me, my covert life came later."

"Let's return to the mother you just mentioned. After you hooked up my sons with that aristocrat of yours—to serve as his henchmen—I had a premonition."

"Hey. They'd finished in the Foreign Legion … I got them jobs."

"You got them killed."

Pattie stood and turned, taking a step to the side as a precaution. It seemed at first glance that the woman in the gown-length crimson dress posed no immediate problem. She'd merely stated a fact.

"Your husband's death wasn't me. He went after the Crayle team on their territory. Lost big time."

"I miss my husband so."

"But you did have a window of opportunity."

"I don't understand."

"With your sons all dead, and before your husband—I believe his name was Remy—ate it, you could've gotten pregnant. Done it all again."

"Clever as always. I did consider it. You must understand why I didn't."

"So, tell me. The Lord can wait."

"My husband and I had the same affliction. In a way, it brought us together. The big jaw. And then our children. Every one. You would not guess, but it played a defining role in all of us becoming criminals."

"Well, a family that crimes together … I'll work on the ending later."

"The deformity actually became a bond. An indelible bond."

"But why no more kids?"

"The life was torturous. I could not do that again. I and my family were all atheists. I've seen the light. I need this God that you worship."

The woman, though quite hardened by life, began to cry.

Pattie stepped close, as would a nun rendering comfort.

"Hold my cross."

She proffered the holy element long leg toward the woman.

The mother of the dead sons and husband took it. In both hands. A look of sincere gratitude graced her countenance.

Pattie hadn't asked how she was tracked all the way from France to Port Arthur, Tasmania. But she did see her future plans suddenly in danger.

She jerked back.

The woman saw that the move had unsheathed a gleaming, double-edge blade, attached to the holy cross.

Pattie lunged.

The blade plunged into the woman's heart as the nun-habited Pattie pulled her latest victim tight.

Dead in that instant, the woman slumped to the floor.

Pattie turned and reassumed her initial position.

"Forgive me, Father … for I have sinned."

• • •

Pattie finished her prayer. Then, she removed her head covering and leaned down to the pool of blood as it spread out from the body. She dipped one of her pigtails. Standing, she faced the eighteenth century beveled glass mirror she'd just pulled from the habit. The silver back-coat had deteriorated over the years. Still, it sufficed.

She smiled, demonstrating her point-dimpled cheeks, appearing child-like. Cherubic. Save for the drips of blood on her left shoulder.

The smile faded as she grasped the inundated pigtail and—in slow motion—pivoted it into her mouth.

"Sylvain would say I'm …" She ran her tongue along her upper lip. "… insane."

She turned to the corpse. "What do you think?"

CHAPTER 38

There was a new and pleasant dawn in Big Bear, California. Former private investigator and current CIA spy, Lenny Lipschitz, felt guilty. He'd escaped performing any real work to restore the Crayle's cabin across the lake from his home. Instead, he boarded his newly-purchased pontoon boat at Holloway's Marina not far from where he lived. The surrey covered boat was top notch. He was certain his wife, Alona, would approve.

A full-speed crossing would ensure the least amount of wave bouncing, he decided. He waved happily at the angry fishermen whose activities he destroyed courtesy of his wake.

He tied up at the Crayle dock, then trudged the fifty feet or so to the cabin.

The eighty-foot pine tree that he and Micmac had worked on the previous day was gone. The split it made in the cabin, gone too. The log sides and roof, fully restored. The shattered windows had been replaced—no doubt with bulletproof, double pane equivalents. In all, it appeared no different than seconds before the drones assaulted the Crayles.

He checked the back door. It's unlocked condition signaled that Micmac must be on site. Lenny decided to announce his presence, lest he place an armed, former SEAL on alert.

"Hey, Micmac. It's me. Wow!"

He glanced around. Nothing out of place. Even Jack Sommers' numerous collector plates adorning the walls, all crushed to bits by the tree's crunch, appeared in perfect shape.

"What's up?" came from behind.

Lenny jumped, then calmed. "I'm so impressed. The instant reset you can perform is reminiscent of what you accomplished in the past."

Micmac touched a button on his collar. "Yo! Team!"

The rest of SEAL Team Six, retired, strode in.

"Team dismissed. Thanks, guys."

The team departed.

Micmac spared Lenny any repercussions should he say the wrong thing.

"Got a comm from Jack. Wanna hear?"

"No, Lenny. You just keep it from me if that's what you want to do. Now. Let me see. Where did I stow the water and the board? And that old, never-washed, mechanic's rag?"

"You wouldn't water board me."

"Actually, no. Got a new method. I've replaced the apprehension of drowning in water with alcohol. Booze Boarding, I call it. I've added that burning sensation to the drowning. Trying various Bourbons, Ryes, and Scotches. For S & T. I've still got Dr. McGillicuddy's Cherry Bomb liquor and Leadslinger's Napalm Cinnamon Whiskey to try. Here, let me get my stuff."

"Jeez-Louise already. I'll tell, I'll tell, I'll tell."

"Yes ..."

"Jack called earlier. I was at the McDonalds getting my fish sandwich. Alona claims fish is good for my health."

"As is staying on her good side."

"Roger that. I've been worried a bit about Magus and Hekka. Since our little to-do's in the American southeast, they've disappeared. Off the grid."

"I just know there's more. Where was my equipment?"

"Okay. Yeah. There's more. President Stones needs Magus back. Apparently, he agreed the Crayles could have time off until their baby drops. Global facial recognition caught them Down Under. New Zealand. Now, he's worried something might *befall* them. He used that word."

"Well, the president always has far more intel than anyone else."

"No one threatens to water board him."

"Let me guess. He asked, or tasked, you to track down Magus with your private investigator skills. Have his back, so to speak. Then, assure that he gets back to D.C. to help the president."

"Nicely done, sailor."

"Phoebe says that."

"She didn't get pregnant by divine intervention." Lenny laughed.

"My government approved special ops watch says ..." He checked. "... your time to tell me the rest is running out."

"Keep a lid on it, as Micmac would say. Oh, that's you." He laughed again.

The former SEAL took one step closer.

The P.I. held up his hands, palms forward. "Jack said the president said for all of us to go. You, me, Alona, and Phoebe. And since our cabin refurb job's obviously done, there shouldn't be a problem. Right?"

"If the two of them are off grid, it's because they want to be. How do we find them? Remember, Magus Number One—of three incarnations—is a trained CIA operative with an assassination merit badge. They don't get much spookier than that."

"That's right. Number Two was the consummate global-redistricting strategist. The Blackstone Strategy he did for Chin was pretty big."

"Consummate? You use that around Alona?"

"She thinks I'm talking dirty. Anyways, Crayle Three is the one we have now, trying to take down the rest of that secret, nuke-using society, Illuminè."

"When do we boogie?"

"Already have the Falcon 7X down the hill at Jack's airport. Out of here in …" He checked his G-Shock watch. "… forty."

"Plenty of time to tell Phoebe that she might not be giving birth to an American. Perhaps a Kiwi or an Aussie."

"Dual citizenship. Great for our next round of spy guys."

"Better make that gals. And take care what you say. Phoebe doesn't need much to want to R.I.P. your sorry ass."

"Noted."

"Let's boogie."

They locked up and left, picked up two less-than-thrilled pregnant wives, and headed down the back side of the Big Bear Valley, past the quarry that housed the CIA's covert hospital deep underground.

The three-engined business jet that Jack Sommers had assigned for their exclusive use arrived on time. They expected to be greeted by their usual pilot, Flori, also Jack's new wife. Instead, the pilot who greeted them wore her trademark bright red lipstick beneath big, black-framed Hollywood sunglasses.

"Marli!" Phoebe exclaimed. "Is Flori inside?"

"I'm it. Newly minted Dassault Falcon 7X pilot."

The four blanched. "You're a realtor."

"Turns out, I can fly and chew gum." She demonstrated the gum chewing.

"Oh."

"It's okay. I've got the usual ex-Top Gun pilot for backup. He'll actually fly the plane … most of the time."

"What's happened to Flori?"

"She's off on a Top Secret mission, in Neil Wohlford's old 8X, no less. Couldn't get the truth, whole truth, and nothing but the truth out of Jack. But, heck. That's why he's my ex."

She handed out passports as they boarded. "As is customary, each one matches you physically. The names and dates-of-birth are new. Memorize. And all visas are in order. Take your seats, ladies and gentlemen, and buckle up. We're going to Auckland, New Zealand. Wheels up."

CHAPTER 39

Even buffeted by an impending storm, the Dassault Falcon 7X touched down with perceptible grace observed by its sole passenger. For Lenny, it accounted for the second leg of the journey. They'd dropped off the baffled other three at Auckland airport to an awaiting limo. Once in the hotel he'd picked for them, he was certain they would forgive him.

Upon taxiing to a full stop, the pilot spooled down its three tail-mounted engines. Marli Sommers exited the flight deck and stepped into the passenger compartment.

Lenny noticed once again that she wore a cleavage-enabled tunic and wasn't at all shy about it.

"Here's the passport that you surrendered prior to takeoff. I've taken the liberty to obtain your Australia entry visa using the CIA developed and hyper secure Ingress App."

"Thanks. This trip was as impromptu as it gets. We spies sometimes make decisions on the fly—and I didn't even consider that I might need a visa."

"Here's an umbrella." She handed it to him.

"Looks like I'll need it. Hope it doesn't flip up in a high wind."

"Actually, it won't. But, it's a product of the Science and Technology Directorate. If you have the need, twist the handle while pushing this button on the bottom."

She demonstrated.

The umbrella canopy flipped itself upward.

"Terrific. Just what I—"

"Watch."

She extracted a cloth from between her breasts and wiped the tips.

"It's a deadly poison. The cloth is impregnated with a neutralizing agent. Push the button again ..." She did. "... and it reverts back to safe mode. Here."

He took it, but his initial thought was to ditch it as soon as he was out of her sight.

"Don't even think that, Mr. Lipschitz. In the wrong hands, it could prove deadly to the innocent."

He deplaned, perilous parasol and Go Bag in hand, and stepped inside an SUV door held open by a very muscular man in a chauffeur's uniform. Apprehensive for the trip ahead, but ready.

• • •

Lenny's arrival at the old tourist park for the Port Arthur Prison was inconsequential except for the heavy rain. The P.I. deployed his umbrella with great care. He skipped the touristy edifice for the other buildings, any one of which could find the Crayles within. Such was the latest facial recognition intel. That they'd first been spotted in Auckland and then not until days later in this place produced a quandary. Questions remained. Where had they been in the interim, and why the intel blackout. He'd learned to be skeptical as a private investigator and then that times ten as a spy on the Crayle team. Did intelligence actually fail, or was someone at Langley or Manassas holding something back?

He proceeded along the walkway until he caught sight of the old church remains. He touched his jacket to reassure himself that his Walther PPK rested in position. He walked inside the roofless ruins.

No one. The place was empty probably due to the downpour. He observed something of interest on the floor. The water that flowed across was being discolored by a red substance. Of course. He recalled times in his earlier days when he'd overloaded his Kosher-compliant all beef hot dogs with ketchup. Some invariably oozed onto his garments in the process of ingesting them, and some squished out on the floor. The obvious conclusion? "Note to self. The Tasmanians definitely enjoyed a good dog."

After nosing around, he was certain that no Crayle evidence was there to be found. His P.I. kit in the Go Bag would be useless with respect to fingerprints. Not in this deluge.

He walked on to another larger building. This time with an operational roof. He stepped inside. A sign informed him that he'd just entered the Separate Prison. As he walked past the heavy cell doors, he heard sounds emanating. The words were a blur, but sounded foreign. Probably Tasmanian. And the "Oh!" from time to time. Surely a couple of the workers were utilizing the absence of tourists to take pleasure as the situation afforded.

Lenny just smiled. If Alona were with him, he might have done the same.

He continued on throughout the site until he'd exhausted any possibility of locating the Crayles, or any artifacts thereof. He found his way back to the jet, Marli, and the flight back to Auckland. There would be some explaining to do, and his crew never seemed to appreciate his efforts unless they produced a major and unexpected success. They were good people, but always seemed to be anticipating an apology from their P.I. colleague. From Lenny. From him.

But not to give up. His father's words hung in his ears. "Never quit." He'd pulled out miracles before. He'd find a way to do it again.

CHAPTER 40

Heading now from Tasmania to Australia aboard the Emerald Princess, the Crayles took a break. They moved inside from the peaceful and relatively quiet Sanctuary to the ship's Wheelhouse Bar. They chose their drinks and were served in short order. Two apiece at this special time.

"Time for a Happy Hour clink." He reached over and tapped her Virgin Rob Roy glass with his Dry Vodka Martini with a twist. Shaken. Not stirred.

"I'm beyond Happy Hour. Beyond Happy Day. Happy Month. And the rest. I'm just Happy."

"Nicely put. Me, too. Australia will be great. Better than that. But, there is a question you must answer correctly to be admitted. Are you ready?"

"You're being silly, and you're only half way through the first martini. Okay. I'll play. Bring on your question."

He sat back as if he'd already won the contest.

"Boy or girl?"

"Magus Crayle! Here you are, spy extraordinaire, and you cannot derive the intel regarding our first child? Let me remind you, you are the usual run-of-the-mill, James Bond-type spy times two." She nodded at the two drinks before him.

"Run-of-the-mill?" His eyebrows lifted.

Hekka took a long look at her husband. Magus Crayle seemed to be at peace with the world. He had procured the best two spots in the ship's forward area called the Sanctuary. She thought back to what they'd just experienced there.

Children yelled, screamed, and cannonballed in a place far away—the large, main pool mid-ship. Integrated into the superstructure and child free, the Sanctuary remained blissfully quiescent.

"Just the sound of the wind and the smell of the sea," Crayle observed. "May there be peace forever."

"My husband the philosopher. Plato?"

"I'll take Yoda." He smiled a pleasant smile.

"We must go to Bondi Beach after we arrive in Sydney. They spoke of it in the lecture I attended, by myself, this morning. It's spelled B-O-N-D-I, but pronounced Bond—as in James Bond—followed by Eye—as in Goldeneye."

"Cute. Like you. But what is Goldeneye?"

"I know that also. The author of the Bond series, Ian Fleming, had a place in Jamaica. He called it Goldeneye. With you becoming a world-famous writer of spy thrillers, we'll have to go stay there someday."

"It seems I've got some work to do."

• • •

A man and a woman sat by their hotel room window with high-powered binoculars and a view of Sydney bay

"Guess who's here, Chapter?"

"I'm trying to sleep, Verse. After last night."

"One of those cruise ships. Wait. I can see a name."

"Those million-dollar CIA specification facial recognition binoculars are not for frivolous operation."

"I'm sure they cost less than that."

"They *are* government."

"It's the Emerald Princess. Wait! They're disembarking passengers."

"Whoop-te-do!"

"And there they are." She checked her Smartphone. "That one's Magus … and the pretty one with the butterscotch-toned flesh is Hekka."

"I feel like an adornment on this mission. The husband to go with the wife." He raised his ringed left hand. "I haven't even been read in."

The man, stocky and mid-sized, pulled one of the thick, hypo-allergenic pillows over his head.

The woman, a perfect wedding cake ornament match for the man, pulled her weapon from its hiding place, and fired two silenced shots through the pillow.

"Sleep tight," she whispered.

CHAPTER 41

The Crayles' prearranged limousine transportation dropped them at Sydney's Hyatt Regency Darling Harbour. As advertised, it sat adjacent to the eponymous harbor. From street side, they saw no harbor, no water, just a regular appearing, nice hotel. Just what they wanted.

Its tall stature implied that, at least in the upper rooms, one would have some grand views of either the city or the waterfront and its endless activity.

A mere twenty minutes later, they checked in. Once ensconced in their nice eighth floor room, they began to feel the magic. Their luggage arrived at almost the same moment they did. It was time to 'take a load off' as Micmac would have opined. They did. On a sumptuous couch.

Hekka plucked a tourist magazine from an end table.

"It says here, Magus, that Australia is a key supplier of precious metals and, oh, diamonds." She checked the stone on her finger.

"And uranium, I hear."

"Oh, dear. Isn't that used to make nuclear bombs?"

"I've detected your facetious tone there. No more hanging out with Lenny."

"No more? As you might recall, I already have a mother to tell me no. But, let me consult my ten-inch Bowie knife just in case it holds the answer."

They broke into a simultaneous laugh. She shook her head in disbelief. "I'm not like that."

"It's stress related. Doctor Magus has brought you to the land down under to relieve your stress … starting now." He stood and removed his clothes.

• • •

An hour later, they showered, dressed, and departed via the hotel's clandestine rear exit. From there, they crossed a nearly hidden street followed by a well-populated area chocked full of diners and revelers.

"Are we eating here?"

"Follow me," Crayle instructed.

He lead her up stairs to a pedestrian-only bridge across the harbor. The views spoke peace and harmony. On the other side, he turned them left into a shopping mall building. Hekka noted a sign.

"Good. We can look for baby clothes. Pink baby clothes."

"We're here for dinner. Clothes later. We're at least a month off from needing baby clothes."

"And you know that how?"

Crayle didn't answer. At the far end of the building he ushered her into the Sydney Hard Rock Café.

• • •

A dinner later, glancing regularly out the window at city lights glinting off the water, he observed. "It's beautiful. But with no breeze to rough up the surface, we don't get our water diamonds sparkling back at us."

"I have the diamond I want."

"And you are my diamond, Hekka. My sparkle. My wealth. Everything."

"That's a bit romantic for a spy."

"But not for your husband. Let's pay up and head back to the hotel. There's something I want to show you."

"Oh, something new?"

He nodded at her tummy. "You've seen it before."

CHAPTER 42

Magus and Hekka Crayle woke to a new day. The morning sun glanced across Darling Harbour only to be thwarted by the drawn, black-out drapes of their eighth floor room.

"If you open them, there'll be no yellow flag tossed for a bright light infraction."

"Nice try, Mr. Crayle. I'm likely the most forgiving woman on the planet. You open them. Besides, it's nice and toasty on this super comfortable bed. We should get one for the cabin."

Crayle stepped to the drapes and pulled them apart.

"Ah!" Hekka pulled the covers over her head. Muffled sounds signaled the triumph of reality over theory.

"Reveille, reveille! Up you get. I've planned our day of peace and tranquility to the minute. Out of here in twenty."

"You're channeling Micmac." She waited a second. "Whine."

"And you're channeling Lenny. C'mon."

He headed for the shower, disrobing as he went.

A grumbling Hekka soon joined him. "No sex in the shower, then?"

He ran his hand over her quite pregnant tummy. "I think there's room for one more."

"Doesn't work that way. Besides, I've analyzed your timeframe. We only have about three minutes for our shower."

"I'm good."

"Not today, Casanova." She re-entered the bathroom, and dropped her towel on the floor.

"Hey. That's the only towel!"

The once-upon-a-time stoic Serrano Indian giggled once again.

Twenty minutes from the first sunlight, they had dressed, descended to the lobby, and departed the hotel via the special secret back door just past the open-concept lobby restaurant.

Once down the stairs, they crossed the narrow, covered street from the night before, but stopped short of the port. Crayle produced a couple of tickets from his jacket pocket.

Five minutes of waiting, and a red, double-decker bus rounded the corner and stopped in front of them. Crayle assisted his wife to board.

"Let's get you upstairs. The day is nice, and fresh air will be good for the baby."

The upper deck was open and only about one-third full of tourists due to the southern hemisphere Spring time of year.

The driver of the Hop-On, Hop-Off mode of transportation called out the city's attractions on either side as he drove. Across the harbor, they saw a cruise ship similar to theirs, but with a different marking on its exhaust funnel, debarking passengers.

"I think I'd like another cruise, Magus."

"One with water tubes to slide down?"

"It's not about the fun and games, or the excellent and abundant food." She took on a serious look. "I hereby declare Peace and Tranquility to be our new middle names."

"Hmmm. Tranquility Crayle. If it's a girl."

"If *she's* a girl."

Their next sight was the famous Sydney Harbour Bridge stretching across to North Sydney. They'd heard someone at the hotel referring to it as the Coat Hanger. It took a little imagination, but yes to coat hanger.

Hekka pointed out a stream of human beings walking on top of the structure. "I won't even consider excitement such as that, or any other, until I've had our baby."

The bus continued through downtown Sydney with fine views of the world famous Opera House and other structural artifacts of the past and present. One bus transfer later, and they reached another world famous aspect of the city, Bondi Beach.

"Off we go," Crayle said at a beachside bus stop. "Gonna get a little lunch at a special place." He'd noticed the sign for Roscoe Street and, since it initiated at the beach road where they stood, there was only one direction to go.

Hekka stood, then nudged him with her elbow. "Been here before, sailor?"

"One. Micmac's the only sailor on our team. Two. I don't know why I remember what I do sometimes, like about this restaurant."

Just another artifact of the CIA-induced amnesia, she thought.

He led them inside. A sign overhead indicated the Hurricane's Grill and Bar – Bondi Beach.

"Indoor," he told the host. "No, outdoor. But under the white canvas sunshades." He nodded toward his wife.

"Yes. We often have requests for women with child to be sheltered from the light."

Crayle recalled Phoebe's conclusion that Lenny was contagious. Apparently, it'd become pandemic.

The pair took their time as they enjoyed a lunchtime repast. They could wander back to the beach, look around, and take a future HOHO bus back toward their hotel on the other side of Sydney. No hurry whatsoever.

• • •

"That was very good. What's next, love?"

"We walk the couple of blocks back to the beach, you take off your clothes, and jump in the water. The rest of us will take social media photos."

"You are so funny."

"It's cool. They'll probably mistake our Baby Inside for a flotation device." He fought back the urge to laugh, rather to maintain the pretence of objective analysis.

In order to take a brief rest, they sat on a short stucco'd wall that separated the sidewalk from the broad beach.

All humor abruptly ended.

A car screeched to a halt.

Three men leapt out, and began shooting randomly.

Spectators scrambled for cover, none of them yet hit.

Crayle wrapped his arm around Hekka, and pulled her over the wall toward relative safety. He flipped them in mid-air so she would land on top. Facing up.

"Oof!" He grunted as they plunked onto the hard-packed sand.

"Don't you say one word about my weight," Hekka warned.

Gently, he set her on the sand.

The gunfire had ceased.

"I'm going to take a peek."

Before she could restrain him, he popped up to eye level, then immediately ducked.

Three rounds ricocheted off the top of the wall, just above their heads. More caught air, finishing in the volatile surf.

"Not good. When I saw them, they were looking right at me."

"Peace and tranquility on hold," Hekka exhausted a breath.

From the north and south ends of the beachside street, a klaxon of sirens blared the arrival of the police.

Crayle peeked once more to see the assailants hop back into their black cars and squeal up Roscoe Street to avoid the police.

"Imagine that. Holden Commodore sedans. They stopped making that brand here back in 2017."

He turned to his wife. To reassure her.

"We're safe!" He helped Hekka to her feet. "Come on! We're safe, but we don't know if these guys have back ups.

They clambered over the wall as the sirens faded into the distance, and just as the next HOHO bus stopped nearby. The driver exited for a potty break.

"C'mon!"

Crayle pulled Hekka onto the bus, planted her in an empty, up front seat, and jumped into the driver's seat.

"I'm hoping bus-jacking isn't a serious crime in Australia."

"I'll call our attorney. Alona will know."

Crayle headed them north. At speed. The police units had already cleared the vicinity. "Now crossing into Dover Heights. Well, that's appropriate. We're on Military Road."

They flew past a very large cemetery.

Just five minutes later, as the double-decker sped through residential and commercial aspects of Sydney, three cars jumped in behind it from side streets. All black. All with dark-tinted windows.

Hekka saw her husband glance into the mirror. She didn't miss the tension it produced on his face. She knew he didn't flex facial muscles unless a situation was exceedingly serious.

"What is it, Magus?"

"The men. At the beach. Same flattop, end-colored hair styles—or lack thereof—of those in the Southeast U.S.A."

"Coincidence?"

"I'm hoping."

"Don't keep it from me. What else did you see?"

"It's just that I thought I noticed one of the cars with a license plate beginning with **Feral**, followed by a single digit."

Neither wanted to contemplate what that might portend.

Soon they raced alongside what was clearly a military base between their street and the harbor.

Crayle swerved the bus right, nearly toppling it over.

A vision of tourists flying from the top deck in all directions crossed his mind.

Bad for business, he thought.

He plowed the bus through the gate, and a guard yelling "Bloody hell!"

To safety.

CHAPTER 43

Jack Sommers had provided intel on Magus Crayle's whereabouts. He'd been electronically spotted by facial recognition in Auckland, New Zealand, on a certain date, not since. It was unknown to the CIA analysts that the Crayles had boarded the Emerald Princess cruise ship, where facial recognition was not available, and that they couldn't be tracked until they departed the ship where such surveillance might once again bear fruit.

"I've made all the arrangements. You guys can go shopping. On Jack's Black Card. Micmac and I will hang out somewhere until we get updated intel on the location of Magus and Hekka. What do you think, Alona?"

"Shopping works. I'm way ahead of you on that one. I checked it out en route. How do we know you two can stay out of trouble?"

"After what just happened," Phoebe added.

"It's like Vegas," Lenny replied. "What happens in the American southeast stays in the American southeast. We're going to jump on the Kiwi version of a Hop On Hop Off bus about a block from here."

"Where does it go?"

"It goes in a circle around Auckland, I think. You get off to see something, then back onto a later one."

"Sounds good. We can shop later." Alona glanced at Phoebe for a reaction. "We're in."

It appeared from Lenny's less than positive reaction that he had yet another unannounced agenda.

The crew got itself ready and walked from the hotel across a narrow roadway past the thousand foot high landmark Sky Tower to the bus stop. Within two minutes, a bright yellow and blue double decker bus with Auckland Explorer Bus on its side in large letters pulled up to take them aboard.

The route had been designed to show off New Zealand's premier city. To that end, it afforded stops such as Bastion Point, a grassy knoll that overlooked the beautiful gulf, harbor, and a quaint, nearby village.

Near the halfway point, the bus lumbered up a topless hill labeled in the literature as Mount Eden. Famous for its elevated city views from the city's highest point, it afforded postcard perfect panoramic vistas.

"We'd like to stop here and take a little rest," Phoebe advised the men. "You go on. We'll run into you here as you make the circle back, or at the hotel."

"You might want to check out Eden Gardens, Phoebs. Let me know if you spot Adam and Eve." Micmac chuckled.

"In our case, that would be Magus and Hekka. Otherwise, you're Adam, I'm Eve. Are we clear?"

Not needing to respond to Phoebe's rhetorical, the men rode the bus down the hill and across town. They spoke nary a word until it stopped at the Eden Park National Stadium.

"Come on, Micmac. This is our stop."

"What do you mean, our stop? Lenny, what are you up to?"

"I got this, man. Via Jack. President Stones scored us tickets to the game of the century."

"What game? What century?"

Micmac followed the diminutive member of the Crayle team off the bus and into the stadium. "What about our ladies, Lenny? I think you're getting us into trouble."

"It's just a game. What could go wrong?"

"Oh, boy."

Shortly, a man approached them holding a cardboard sign that said, "Lipschitz Party."

"Well, check this out. It's that special, personalized treatment you'd only expect in airports. The president is definitely my man."

"Ask the guy which way to the baggage carousels."

The nice man showed them to their special seats, though Lenny caused a commotion climbing over people who'd done their best to allow passage. Some jerked away as he passed. It seems that the chili he'd eaten earlier wasn't agreeing with him.

Lenny tried to gain favor by crying out, "Go Kiwis!" It would've gone better had they not been traversing a section of die-hard Aussie rugby fans.

Having taken their seats between opposing fans, the din in the stadium indicated that the Game Of The Ages, as it had been promoted, would begin momentarily.

CHAPTER 44

To the background strains of Dire Straits' famous tune, Sultans Of Swing, a man at mid-field stepped right up to a microphone. As he did, an armed guard marched out from an under-the-grandstands tunnel. Between two lines of armed military and police guards drawn from the two countries' finest, a souped up golf cart transported what appeared to be the game ball. The announcer put the display in context.

"Good afternoon, ladies and gents."

Uproarious applause broke out.

When the din depleted to half volume, he continued.

"Today's game ball, the one you can see making its way to the center of the field, is no ordinary ball. It is, in fact, the very ball from the first ever rugby championship between our very own All Blacks and the Aussie National Rugby Union team. That is correct, my fellow Kiwis. The Wallabies."

His information was greeted with thunderous applause. A standing ovation honored the entourage as it stopped, and the speaker held the ball aloft.

"It has been closely guarded all these years, but has been brought out of retirement on this momentous anniversary of that seminal game in 1903."

More yells and hoots, and some singing ensued.

He placed it on the center line of the rugby pitch.

The guard unit retreated to the sideline.

Curious, Lenny pulled binoculars from his backpack. He placed the strap around Micmac's neck, then yanked them to his own eyes to take a look.

"Hey!" Micmac yelled as the motion yanked his head to one side.

Lenny ignored him. "I'm checking out the ball and … oh … me … no … not at all good!"

"What?"

"That ball! It's got one of those whatchamacallits wrapped around! One of those coatings!"

"What coatings?" Micmac reached for the binoculars, but Lenny held him off.

"The honeycomb material. The one the Chinese put on their—"

"The radiation sponge? On the mini-nukes?"

"Call the girls. Tell 'em to stay on Mount Eden. Don't hop on cause the bus would come this way."

Micmac wrenched the binoculars away. He looked. "Omigod!" He ran to the entrance tunnel so he could be heard over the Smartphone. Purposefully, he dialed down his excitement.

"Alona! It's Micmac! Don't get on the bus! Find cover! There's a bomb at the stadium!"

"What stadium? A bomb?"

"Mini-nuke, it looks like, at Eden Park Stadium. We're there!"

He heard her tell Phoebe, who tapped the Speaker icon.

"Get outta there!"

"You two get down into that meteor-caused crater that the driver pointed out. I'll grab Lenny. Love you!"

Micmac ran back prepared to traverse the throng of yelling, singing, screaming, and foot-stomping fans.

He checked. His and Lenny's seats were empty.

Then, the crowd pointed to the field. There. He saw a small man running to the center of the playing field between the two lines of the most virile athletes on the planet.

"Lenny!" Micmac yelled in vain. "No!"

Not a chance in hell Lenny could hear. He'd commandeered a zip line that led from the stadium top to the playing surface.

Lenny reached mid-field, grabbed the rugby ball, tossed it in the back of the golf cart, and drove away at top speed.

A stadium full of rabid fans, the two teams, and the dumbstruck master of ceremonies were, at first, shocked.

When the culprit his own wife referred to as 'the twerp' absconded with the item of near religious significance, the rest took off in pursuit.

Lenny, his life in danger for two reasons, sped away from his blood-thirsty pursuers.

It didn't help when Micmac cried out. To warn the crowd. "*Bomb! There is a nuclear bomb!*"

In the few seconds following, as fans sat immobile and with mouths gaping, some recovered enough to spread the word. What the man had shouted was too insane to be true. And if it were, it would surely be somewhere else. Not here. Not today.

Micmac used the paralysis he knew to be temporary in panic situations, and he made a bee line out of the stadium. A great plan. The only plan. Until guards at the front gate stopped him.

With the uproar of tens of thousands of irate, blood thirsty fans behind him, and the tall fence and guards in front, he felt trapped. He readied his mind for combat.

The lead guard addressed him with a quizzical look. "Hey, mate. You can't leave now. The game's not even on yet. You can't miss this one."

Micmac considered taking on five armed and no doubt trained men so he could escape. Okay, he said to himself. Whenever a violent solution can't work, try diplomacy. "I got a call, mate. Need to get home to the pregnant misses. She'd forgotten to tell me that some old chums from my Navy days arrived as a surprise."

The guard nodded his understanding. "I served as well."

"Gotta get off and throw a shrimp on the barbie, you know."

"Understand." The guard turned to his compatriots. "Let 'im pass."

Two of the others opened the gate, and Micmac exited quick as he could. It surprised him how well his fake Australian accent had worked, especially in a stress situation. He'd been unsure of that, but of one other thing he was definitely sure. He intended to locate and throw one particular shrimp on the barbie.

Lenny.

He jerked out of his burgeoning scheme by the HOHO bus as it arrived across the street. Quick as he could, he hopped on and grabbed the first available seat near the front door.

As the bus departed, his jaw dropped. There on a grassy field not far away sat the ceremonial Golf Car Lenny had used for his getaway.

Micmac spun in his seat.

Lenny sat three rows back.

That the P.I. wore a smile irritated him. That the P.I. had a backpack on his lap with a rugby ball sized telltale bulge in it, horrified him.

CHAPTER 45

It was later that day. It must have been. There he was. He and his wife had just visited the revolving restaurant, Orbit 360, in the Auckland Sky Tower. On a dare, Lenny stepped outside onto the narrow Skywalk strip. A thin, strap tether was all that would keep him, in theory, from a 1,076-foot plunge.

The air, crisp and blowing, kept him wide awake. Why had he bet Micmac, the consummate gadget man, that he couldn't do what he obviously could. Mick MacKay had managed a cable between the Auckland Sky Tower and the similar Sydney Sky Tower. Here was Lenny, who'd laughingly agreed to try the world's longest zip line. A mere 1,341 miles. He'd allowed that it didn't sound as bad as the 2,158 kilometer equivalent.

Just inside behind him in the heavy viewing window, Alona pounded viciously. He read her lips. "Don't you dare!"

He turned and uttered, "For God and country!" Then, he jumped.

The next thing he remembered, he'd slammed into something very hard. Not the base of the far away Australian tower. The floor next to his bed.

"Lenny! Are you all right!" Alona yelled.

"I'm okay. Just a nightmare." He planned to have a word with Micmac when he saw him next.

He picked himself up, just as his phone rang.

"Please turn that damn thing off! Our baby and I are trying to sleep!"

Lenny ignored her and isolated himself in the bathroom.

"This is Heidi," said the voice.

"You'd gone dark. I worried they'd gotten you."

"It was close. Listen, we don't have much time. Meet me …"

Lenny noted carefully what he needed to do. She'd arranged a tour for the Lipschitzes. A place on his bucket list. The Lord Of The Rings Hobbiton site not far south of Auckland. Alona would never suspect. He'd get this all done in the idyllic setting, and would re-earn the trust of the team.

They'd be picked up in the lobby.

• • •

The large air conditioned tour bus was on time as was suggested in the on-line rating entities. After a quite long ride south through the countryside, the signs started popping up indicating that they were close. They gave the impression that Hobbits were indeed real.

Alona felt quite comfortable, considering the advanced nature of her pregnancy. The roads, at least in this part of New Zealand's North Island, were quite well maintained. The coach didn't bump or sway, and all the visuals were peaceful ones.

"I should be writing this down," Lenny said. "I could present this to Magus as intel."

"Why is it that he would need intel?"

"For his next book. Or the one after that. I don't know."

"What if he doesn't want to write about this country? With his memories restored, he probably has plenty of material for all the books he might write."

"He told me that all of his previous experiences help. They provide the fodder for his locations, his characters, and the thrills."

"And how does he get all that?"

"From what he's done. All the places. All the people. All the action."

"Wherever he and Hekka are at this moment, you can bet that action is the last thing on their minds, books or not. Hekka told me that love, peace, and understanding need to be it from here on out."

The bus completed the trip and all the tourists stepped off. They headed out on their tour amongst the washboard rolling hills with the little Hobbit habitats embedded in them, here and there.

Despite warning signs to the contrary, about halfway through the tour, Lenny poked inside one of the movie residences.

He quickly popped back out. "Come on in, Alona. I'd like you to meet Frodo."

She thought it was some kind of tour gimmick. She complied.

Outside, the tour moved on to other parts of the movie location.

Inside, Alona saw what Lenny had been talking about.

"Good morning, Mrs. Lipschitz. I'm Frodo. And the one standing next to me is Sam."

"That's very nice. I'm glad to meet you."

But something didn't seem right. She'd been an attorney for a long, long time, and she had developed a virtual sense of smell. When something didn't smell right, it seldom was.

"We'll not bore you with stories or movie trivia … or anything else," said the Frodo lookalike. "What we'll do is this."

Both produced handguns.

Sam poked his head out the door and scanned the landscape to assure there were no dawdling tourists outside, then secured the door.

"It turns out that there is someone who wishes to meet you."

He turned to Lenny.

"Do not resist, Mr. Lipschitz. And your wife and child will continue unharmed."

Lenny, so centered on the man, failed to observe the other pressing a hypodermic into his wife's arm.

As she fell to the floor, the worried P.I. dropped to his knees beside her. Then, the second needle scored its mark.

CHAPTER 46

A new dawn arrived in Sydney, Australia.

"You want to finish closing those black out drapes?"

Micmac stared at his wife from his seat at the hotel's rendition of a work desk. He knew he couldn't tell her about the events of the previous day. Where their long time team mate and friend, Lenny, had taken him to the Game Of The Century in order to commit the Crime Of The Century. He didn't need to check with attorney Alona to understand that Down Under, stealing the ancient game ball at a rugby match brought with it the death penalty. All trial privileges would be waived, and any appeals would take place long after the execution of perps Mick MacKay and Lenny Lipschitz.

Fact was, he hadn't heard a peep from the P.I. since they'd hopped on the HOHO the day before, barely escaped with their lives, and then hopped back off near the Sky Tower. They'd padded the short distance to their hotel in short order, collars up, and looking down to avoid detection. Just in case any of the thousands of phone cameras had caught them in the act.

No one seemed to take notice, although he assumed everyone on the planet owned a Wanted Dead or Alive photo of Lenny.

When he awakened at 3:35 A.M., he considered arranging for the next flight out of Auckland, however that might manifest itself. If Flori wasn't standing by with the Falcon 7X, then it needed to be commercial. Any class would do. Just get me out of here, he thought. And my very pregnant wife, Phoebe. But then, yesterday had no doubt been a one shot deal. He had a plan for the day, and it included his wife.

"The drapes?" pulled him from his dream state.

He jumped up and strode to the window. "No can do. Sailors work in the daylight."

Phoebe knew what came next. She pulled the pillow over her head.

"Reveille, reveille," came in a loud voice. Micmac yanked apart the drapes. "All hands on deck. Commence ship's work."

"Where's my Glock?" came the muffled words.

"Forget the weapon. Last night you told me about what you and Alona saw yesterday and wished you could've shared it with me. Well, I have good news. We're doing the HOHO this morning. Mount Eden, here we come."

"Oh, whine. Where are Lenny and Alona, anyway?"

"Today it's just us, sweetheart. Just us."

The former SEAL allowed that the Lipschitzes would likely sleep until noon or were already off to someplace on their own. He knew the P.I. well. They'd be back by dinner time. He would see to it that he and his wife were back by then so they could share a nice repast. Perhaps at the tower's revolving restaurant.

He led her across a narrow roadway and past the Auckland Sky Tower to the bus stop. Just eight minutes later, they'd boarded the Hop On Hop Off vehicle for a circle tour of the city's surrounds. A half hour later, the bus stopped at Mount Eden.

"You'll have to walk a bit. They've that little roadway up the hill that is forbidden to vehicles."

As the two alighted, Micmac tipped the driver, then led Phoebe up the gentle hill.

"There's that crater I mentioned yesterday. Don't get too close. I grabbed a little intel off the Web. That symmetric depression to our left is 150 feet deep. It was caused by a meteor, I think. It's sacred, or a person could step down those narrow terraces the aboriginals cut into the sides. Cool, huh?"

Phoebe's breath became somewhat labored, but the on-loan-to-the-CIA FBI agent refused to show any weakness. "Yeah. Cool."

At the top of the road's leftward arc, they took in the panorama of the large city.

"When Lenny gets us our share of the diamond money, we just might buy a place here in New Zealand."

"I've heard both islands are beautiful. We'll have to explore."

"Since we're alone up here, there's something I'd like to explore."

"Whoa, baby. Take it easy, gal. We need to get to know each other first."

"At least I didn't say, Hey, Sailor."

A 'Hey, Sailor' did come from behind them. Micmac and Phoebe turned to a couple of men with handguns. They appeared out of nowhere.

CHAPTER 47

The fact that his office was three hundred feet underground didn't phase Jack Sommers. The insulation was sufficient that he barely heard the rumble at the Manassas, Virginia, Civil War battlefield national park above when they lit off a few of the cannons for the tourists.

What really bothered him was the chartreuse wall paint his predecessor had commandeered from the 'don't use this under any circumstance' government vaults.

Two more Tylenols, and he'd be fine.

His phone rang. It was ***that*** ring.

"Hello, Mr. President. I mean, Kimbel. I'm sorry. I've got protocol of the brain these days. How can I help you?"

"Don't fret about the name calling. As I told you long ago, both are just fine."

"I'm glad to hear that. Running an outpost in northern Greenland isn't on my bucket list. What do you need?"

"A sitrep, Jack. A global sitrep. I'm tight on schedule today. Meeting with three heads of state … separately."

"I'm a real Boy Scout, Kimbel. Prepared."

"I had a steak for breakfast that was well prepared. Go ahead."

"Jump in anywhere you feel the need. Presidential privilege and all."

"Deal. Go."

"Well, the television news this morning carefully noted a quite serious situation Down Under. The aboriginals had planned a major congregation, conference, and religious ceremonies—commitment to have their own country—and it was going to occur at the Australian Red Centre. Coming to the big red-hued monolith known to the rest of the world as Ayers Rock. And known to them, the native population, throughout the ages. Going to Ulurú. Interesting situation brewing down there.

"But that news had been pushed aside due to a near-crisis situation in New Zealand. Perhaps the biggest rugby game ever had been set to take place in Auckland. Tickets scalped for thousands of local dollars above the printed price, and that was if you could even find one.

"The stadium at Eden Park had been packed to the rims. That they'd placed security quadruple that for a normal contest didn't stop some maniac from descending onto the field, stealing the very special game ball, and disappearing into the city. The media continued to report that the thief, a diminutive man, and described by some as sallow—perhaps dementedly so—was the perpetrator.

"To the present moment, none of the local or other law enforcement agencies could identify him, had any idea to his whereabouts, or the location of the relic and, in many ways priceless, rugby ball. No motive could even be imagined for such a horrific and heinous crime.

"It was noted by one station that, at least, the most important of all relics of religious significance, Ulurú, was perfectly safe and immobile. There in Australia's Red Centre for eternity."

"What else?"

"Dateline: Sweden—"

"You found my backstory somewhere. That I'd spent time as a reporter. Out on the coast near your homestead."

Jack smiled into the phone. And began again.

"Dateline: Sweden. That Lalumière kid, Jean-Marc, and the Queen now reside together at the Stockholm Royal Palace. Word is that they plot for, and need, to have the new pope pronounce Sylvain and Pattie Lalumière, who were all prepped to become King and Queen of France, dead. It's my guess they would have the pontiff proclaim and crown Jean-Marc as their rightful successor. As you are aware, the French government, formerly in exile, all dead at Xian trying to make a save-the-day treaty with Chin."

"I don't understand. How does Jean-Marc get in?"

"Our intel indicates that Jean-Marc has a video of the secret marriage of his father and Pattie at the Roman Colosseum. Jean-Marc is in line to have France, and his Swedish queen and lover, already has Sweden. They plan to marry after Jean-Marc becomes king. Accomplishing that, they would unite the kingdoms of France and Sweden."

"Could you whip up a little more intrigue?"

"No sweat. What if Lalumière is alive? And what if he possesses the Black Diamond, the one item that guarantees succession to the throne of France?"

"The Swedish Queen has dumped all of the socialists onto the political scrap heap. She's made it a point that the Swedish government will no longer ... what's that old song line ... 'rob the rich, to feed the poor, 'til there are no rich no more, where will we be?' "

"I'm glad you didn't sing that."

"Related to all this is that the French people are being prepared for the Son of Mitim. Remember our team chasing him and Pattie around Europe?"

"Do I. I'm thinking of declaring war on those mini-nuclear devices. Hey. Forget that. A war to end all wars. My legacy."

"Good try, Kimbel. We've had those before. They don't work. The people in charge just use war as an opportunity to develop new and filthier weapons."

"If I wanted filthy, I'd watch daytime TV. Look. I'm nearly out of time. What else do you have?"

"Dateline Russia. Vladimir and the czarina appear to be an item. Before Old Vlad headed off to Moscow, he met with her at Catherine's Palace near Saint Petersburg. Seems the two spent more than a little time at the palace. It also seems that Catherine's renowned sexual proclivities were infectious still. A little fly on the wall—one of our bugs, actually—tells us they discussed Vlad's plan to become royal—the czar—as the czarina ascended the throne. I'm thinking it would then be child's play—if the child were a sociopath—to have the czarina killed, and blame the old Moscow hardliners, one of which he'd been. It could work. Anyway, every time he went into the bathroom to muse out loud, she took him back to bed."

"Quickly, Jack."

"Dateline China. Empress Ling has the former communist government's Standing Committee doing her bidding. She thinks. Other players are the old Yellow and White daughters of Chin Yao-wu. Seems White's pregnant with Chin's kid. The kid becomes emperor, if he lives. My money is that Ling takes her out to eliminate the threat.

"Outside of Hong Kong, the various regions become ever more selfish, even resisting the Ling governance. Ruling China is a challenge, Kimbel. If she lets the baby be born, the role of dowager empress might look better than what she has now."

"Best for last, Jack. Illuminé?"

"No telling. Our intel on them has gone black. Haven't been able to spot Lalumière, if he's still alive. Best to get Magus back in operation. He's the expert on all things Illuminé."

"I'm glad things are so straightforward and simple. I wouldn't say this to anyone but you, but I long for those far more dangerous, but far less complicated days I had at the NSA. Oh, well. Gotta run.

Thanks. Look forward to your next sitrep. And, Jack. If you need anything, and I mean anything, ask. Okay? Seriously, my man."

The president rang off.

Jack sat back.

He didn't recall what the words *less complicated* even meant.

CHAPTER 48

From the military base in Sydney where they'd escaped the Ferals, the Crayles flew via military transport to Ayers Rock Airport, otherwise known as AYQ.

Flying in the fashion they did assured they would keep their weapons. A sign on the airport terminal wall indicated that having them might be a good idea.

Be Prepared for Dingoes and Wild Dogs.

Besides English, the warnings were explained in two other European and one Asian language. What happened to persons not fluent in those seemed unpleasant to contemplate.

With potential airport inspections and their consequences no longer at issue, the two on-leave American spies were shown to the standard white, black, and red AAT Kings shuttle bus for the brief trip to the Ayers Rock Resort.

They hopped the free transportation to their next place of temporary residence, the Desert Gardens Hotel, all arranged to perfection by their new Australian comrades. Quickly into their room to minimize risk of airborne detection, they were struck immediately by a view through their window. It appeared as would a huge, basaltic loaf of mid-red bread, fallen from the heavens to embed itself in what Australians referred to as the Red Centre of the country. They observed its beauty for a full fifteen minutes without a word spoken.

The silence was broken by the doorbell. Crayle answered.

"Yes. Mr. and Mrs. Crayle?" said a shortish, uniformed man. "I am to escort you to your tour."

Nonplussed, they followed the man to a nearly full bus and were on their way.

The man who'd plucked them from their room, also the driver, gave a running dialog as the bus skirted the periphery of the rock. He then pulled up to a circular building—formally, the Ulurú Cultural Centre—perhaps thirty feet in diameter.

"We'll alight here for one half hour," the guide told them. He gave them a time certain to be back on the bus. Otherwise? Wild dogs and dingoes?

Inside, the Crayles wandered around, checking out artifacts of the aboriginal inhabitants of the area. They read about the seminal people's reverence for the rock. A notice on the wall admonished visitors to refrain from climbing on the rock due to its religious significance. It didn't say ***Or Else***, but one got the message.

"We have some time, let's do a potty break."

Crayle nodded. They parted.

Once back into the room, both noticed the absence of their tour group.

Crayle checked his watch. "We've got time left. I'll check outside."

Before he could move, the entire building shook.

"Earthquake, I think," Hekka said.

"Quick. We've had them in Big Bear before. It's best if we just sit until it's over."

The building continued to move, as if sinking into the soil.

Approximately forty feet down, it stopped.

In through the door walked, not the driver or any of the other tourists, but a man in khaki shorts and shirt—and twenty other men.

Memories of times just past struck the Crayles. The men all sported flat top haircuts with a variety of color highlights. A veritable rainbow of deadly operatives.

"These," the man began with a distinct Australian accent, "are Ferals. And I? I am Farrell. Hamilton Farrell to be precise. Feral and Farrell. A quite cute play on words, wouldn't you say?"

The pair let the rhetorical slide. There was, at the moment, far too much to process.

"Please. Follow me." He led them outside the building.

They observed that they now stood in a circular hub. Large, dark tunnels pushed through the red rock in three directions. The ambient color brought back memories of the caverns far beneath the fairy tale castle in southern Bavaria. The cave with the embedded rubies.

A set of upscale, electric golf carts—Golf Cars, actually—transported them through the dimly lighted earthen tube to its far terminus.

"Please," the man said in a measured tone. "Take a seat over there."

With twenty firearms pointed at them, they obeyed. They sat on two chairs positioned in a quite unimpressive room just beyond the tunnel opening.

Crayle was beside himself. From visiting a cultural marvel to captives in a few seconds. He glared at the man responsible.

"What just happened is beyond comprehension. Beyond reason, logic, the whole long list. I'm betting you're about to clue us in. Am I right?"

"But of course, Mr. Crayle. To those few who even know of us, our Illuminé worldwide secret organization appears to be a snake without a head. It was, however, a snake with two heads. With the Elder turned to hot ash in the Monte Carlo nuclear explosion, I became the sole leader. Not merely manipulating the Southern Hemisphere as before ..." He elevated his chin. "... but now the entire world."

his own partners in crime, the Aryans. I know. I was in Beijing when the mini-nuke detonated in the Underground City. Xian, likewise."

"Not credible, Mr. Crayle. You would be quite dead in either case."

Crayle remembered the explosion in Beijing's Underground City, a purpose-built, Cold War style nuclear bomb shelter. He also remembered the massive burial mound of China's first emperor, Ch'in Xihuangdi, that saved he and his team from the air burst over the ancient capital of Xian. The one that took the most recent emperor, Chin Yao-wu.

"Nothing can stop us. Nothing can stop me."

"Empress Ling now runs China. And leaderless France is also beyond your reach."

"I, and Illuminé, have the capacity beyond the small nuclear devices of which you are so familiar. Come watch."

He led Crayle into a rustic at best dining area. Boomerang-shaped remote in hand, he closed the drapes. Another button extended the table to become a horizontal, high-resolution video screen.

Crayle recognized a large university.

"It's Berkeley, Mr. Crayle. University of California at Berkeley, to be precise."

Crayle observed.

"As you can see, there is a multitude of buildings with no two alike. Perhaps to denote creativity. Near the Life Sciences buildings ..." He pointed with the remote. "... lies an open area bounded by the Near West Circle and the Free Speech Bikeway. There, students mill about or move between classes, or into and out of the dining commons. Not far away, you will observe students in larger numbers than usual populating the Eucalyptus Grove and the Gateway aspects of the campus."

"Is there a point here with reference to Illuminé?"

"Watch."

He pressed down on the remote, and video buttons appeared at the right end of the screen.

ASSEMBLE – PROTEST – RIOT

He touched the first and the screen divided into forty sections, each showing a classroom.

"These are from the soft sciences, as they say. No hard ones such as the Mathematics that you studied. No Physics. No Chemistry. Instead, Sociology, Political Science, and so forth."

Students checked their iPads and Smartphones, rose together, and filed into the square.

Crayle didn't know what to make of it. And the students didn't just leave, mid-class. They threw books and overturned tables and chairs.

By the time they reached the collection area, they had popped out push-button protest signs—created so as to appear hand written. They appeared to operate like push-button umbrellas. A clever device Crayle knew that the gadget man, Micmac, would appreciate.

The Aussie touched a second screen button, and the students began to chant and waive the signs.

"How ..."

"Watch them."

He tapped **RIOT**.

Simultaneously, five of the students withdrew bottles from their back packs, lit rags stuffed into the openings, and threw their Molotov Cocktails at the buildings nearby.

"The campus police have arrived, as you can see, but have orders to merely observe the mayhem. At this very moment, other students are assaulting the police headquarters in Sproul Hall."

"Surely the campus police and the local law enforcement ..."

"No, Mr. Crayle."

Crayle stopped. The shock of it all had rippled through. "Of course. The police chiefs!"

"Illuminé."

"The university chancellor?"

"The same."

The Aussie produced an insidious-looking sardonic grin.

"The mayor?"

"Illuminé."

"The governor of California?"

The Aussie nodded.

Crayle, stymied by what he'd just witnessed, considered its implications.

"Surely not the new American president?"

"When your friend moved up to replace the death-by-suicide former president, a new vice president was installed. Hazard a guess as to her loyalties?"

The spy consumed the intel. "Then you'll …"

"Soon, Mr. Crayle. Soon. When we rid ourselves of Kimbel Stones."

A moment passed.

"Oh, I almost forgot." He pressed a key on the remote.

The video scrunched the Berkeley campus scene onto the left half of the video table. The right side now sported a through-the-windshield view of the campus entrance. Below, the face of a tan-skinned man with a dark, full beard.

The Aussie pointed his remote at the image, and pressed a button.

"Fast-forward, Mr. Crayle."

Under remote control, the accelerator mashed to the floor.

Terrified, the man in the vehicle slammed his foot onto the brake pedal with both feet.

Nothing.

He repeated and repeated.

Nothing.

"Fly by wire systems have replaced the mechanical connections of old."

The car slammed into the crowd.

Bodies flew.

"Oh, I forgot to introduce you. That is—or was—Abdul. Saudi royal family. In the states to study. Political Science, I believe."

Crayle understood the extreme nature of his enemies. It wasn't just take over this country or that country, it was global sedition. And who was going to stop them?

"How do people like you turn into monsters, Farrell? Were your parents evil, too?"

"I am so alike them and so different. You may wonder why I have a crucifix ensconced in a wall-mounted display case."

"It is curious. As Illuminé, you are, by definition, an atheist."

"I've engaged in a transformation of sorts. My sense of virtue, with all the Catholic guilt instilled by my father, has affected a 180-degree shift. I had help. It occurred on an overseas trip."

"Your well-developed virtue disappeared?"

"No. Not disappeared. Just transitioned a great deal."

"So, not a loss of virtue, rather a Virtue Transition."

The Australian reacted as if inspired.

"Nicely put, Mr. Crayle. Yes, a virtue transition. It rather sounds like a book title." He swept his right hand, palm outward, in front and at arm's length. "The Virtue Transition. What do you think, Mr. and Mrs. Crayle? With a capital T and a capital V. With intrigues. With global politics. With, hmmm, with spies."

The Aussie turned to the two as if exiting a trance. He emitted a brief chuckle. "You aren't spies, are you, Mr. and Mrs. Crayle?"

CHAPTER 49

The room was cold, damp, and dingy. A number of mudded over windows to the outside admitted no sunlight. Only man-made lighting in the distance cast any manner of visual recognition of the surroundings.

In the room's center, two individuals sat restrained in a pair of plastic and metal chairs. The fasteners were tight and, since they'd been in place for quite some time, painful.

The sole door creaked open, allowing three men to walk inside. A pair of muscular men stepped forward and snapped the black hoods off their captives, who gasped when they saw their captors.

The two men took up positions on each side of them. Blonde with blue-tipped flattops. Ferals.

The third man, also an Australian, was obviously in charge. His demeanor and swept back longish hair style gave him away. He nodded to one of his men.

The Feral stepped behind an irritated Lenny, and placed a braided metal garrote around his neck, pulling it just snug.

"I'm not telling you anything. I'm not … I'm not …"

The device tightened. The P.I. choked in a near panic response.

The Aussie nodded. His man removed the strangulation device from Lenny's neck, and moved over to Alona, whose heart already raced. He applied the weapon to her neck, a slight bit tighter.

Lenny heard her desperate gasps. He knew he had to change the subject, whatever it was.

"All right, all right. Tell me about your mine."

"My mine isn't at issue, Mr. Lipschitz. You are." He nodded once more.

The Feral slacked off the garrote, allowing it to drop onto Alona's collar bones. Ready in an instant to reapply.

"It was I who purchased the one pound bag of perfect one-carat diamonds via my intermediary in Amsterdam. Your presence here leads me to believe that your private investigator credentials are what brought you to our Down Under. Am I right?"

Not wanting to admit that his arrival Down Under had been only in search of the Crayles, he replied, "That's right, eff-head! And there are more following my lead."

"As his attorney …" Alona started.

"He won't be requiring a solicitor, Mrs. Lipschitz. Nor will you."

It was clear in short order that the two before him would not be supplying much in terms of the intelligence he required. But, they might be of use later. "Let them be," he said. "Watch them carefully. Listen to nothing they say. These seemingly innocuous types can be very clever. Especially the females. I'll move on in my quest to understand just what sort of operation is going on."

He closed the old door so abruptly when he left, that a pane of glass shattered onto the stony ground outside.

• • •

The ride to his second mine took a mere twenty minutes over the rough terrain. Down inside he brought a second pair of Ferals into a dilapidated office. He hoped to break his other captives down and actually obtain useful information.

The Aussie walked over to face the MacKays. Like the Lipschitzes, they'd been tethered to inexpensive chairs, the sort that stacked nicely for easy deployment whenever an opportunity for an impromptu interrogation arose. He decided to try a less aggressive approach.

"Good morning, Mr. and Mrs. MacKay. It's so nice having you as my guests."

Before he could speak further, Phoebe vented.

"Handguns at twenty feet," the FBI superstar spat at her captor. "Naw, let's do fifty."

"Your Annie Oakley celebrity status at the Bureau, as it is referenced by insiders, is well known, Mrs. MacKay. Or may I call you Phoebe?"

Micmac interjected. "When you choose what to call her, consider the words with care. They might be your last."

"I was gonna say that," Phoebe followed.

The Aussie smiled. Feeling he was in total control and beyond reach permitted him to do that. "Let me show you around."

He stopped to observe them bound hand and foot with heavy duty Velcro to the pair of chairs. "Oh, don't get up." He raised his hand as if interrupted by an epiphany. "Since you cannot follow me around, I shall lead you on a verbal tour. And please listen respectfully. I do like to point out my successes."

They said nothing.

"First, there's my gold mine. Officially, Mine Number 1. I say that in reality, but also in euphemistic terms. It was my first effort. I did my homework. I worked hard. The Christian ethic, you know."

He inhaled deeply, then let it go. He'd have to leave out so much. So very, very much. The lecture continued.

"I struck gold. And with the proceeds, created the other two mines in succession not far from here. The second you would appreciate. Number 2 provides the raw diamonds. They are proffered and sold in Rotterdam. The cash from those sales then proceeds to a respected diamond merchant in Amsterdam, where it is translated into precious, perfect stones. The world's underground currency. Squeaky clean. Impressed?" He glanced around.

Phoebe and Micmac knew about Amsterdam. Lenny's half brother, Wolfie, had begun work in a diamond brokerage there. Before one Pattie Norbrunn murdered him.

The Aussie continued. "It's all right. I don't require applause. But I am the best at what I do."

Micmac bit his lip so hard, it bled. He really wanted to explain to the three prospective corpses in the room how the new modern criminal currency ought to be crypto. However, helping an arch criminal avoid detection had a negative moral aspect to it. He kept quiet.

The impatient Aussie shook his head. He felt he'd just traversed two more stepping stones toward his goal. He nodded to the Ferals.

"Ouch!" Phoebe cried out.

Micmac reacted with an "Oh!" to the same needle behind *his* left ear.

• • •

Hamilton Farrell travelled to the last mine. He noted that the final pair no longer struggled against their bonds. Good, he thought. Capitulation. A stack of mined materials sat nearby under a blanket of thin, lead-infused material.

He stepped from his electric vehicle to face the illustrious Magus Crayle. He'd already noted that the pregnant woman next to him sat in increasingly severe discomfort.

"I'm terribly sorry for your seating arrangement. It seems that, physically unrestricted, you each present a near and present danger to anyone in your path. Especially you with that short sword, Mrs. Crayle."

"It's a Bowie."

"Yes, of course. Named after the American patriot, James Bowie."

"Jim Bowie," Hekka corrected.

"You should appreciate this one. Shaft Number 3, behind you, leads from this mine, Number 3. It's the final member of my mining empire, Mr. Crayle. Uranium. The substance of which nuclear power stations are fueled. And, of course, nuclear bombs. I have a business association I'm sure you will appreciate. With someone you know. A Miss Ling An-yee has assisted me in transforming this raw material into miniature nuclear weapons. But you already are familiar with them, aren't you?"

Farrell observed Crayle deep in thought. And perhaps, regret.

Crayle knew all about the young empress of China. He'd first met her as one of Chin Yao-wu's adopted daughters as he'd helped the stock market mogul plan a grand takeover of his country.

"I shall continue. When last I visited with her, she informed me. It was you who devised the entire plot for my organization. Your Blackstone Strategy laid out the sequence of events by which our Illuminé could utilize these very powerful yet compact weapons as the means to create a world empire. For that you have my gratitude. See here. I know you've both had a quite trying day. For now, good night Mr. and Mrs. Crayle."

The Australian nodded to a woman standing behind his secret society's primary adversaries.

A sharp pin prick turned out the lights for the Crayles. Just before they passed out, they heard the Aussie say, "Don't worry. I can assure you that we are not finished."

With them sedated, he had a final word. "You'll have to excuse me. I have other guests to process in. I assure you, Madame, that the sedative chosen will not harm your baby."

• • •

Upon their recovery from an unconscious state, Magus and Hekka Crayle were transported back down the tunnel to the central hub. They and their chairs were placed next to one another, and facing away from the path they'd just taken.

The ever present Australian addressed them once again.

"I can see from your expression that you fully comprehend the magnitude of my power. Of our power. Allow me to demonstrate something on a lesser scale."

Farrell held up a Smartphone, and touched the screen.

The Cultural Centre elevated to surface level. Then, back down.

"I love gadgets, Mr. and Mrs. Crayle, somewhat as does your own gadget man." He nodded to one of the Ferals.

Five more stepped from a second tunnel, which also emptied into the fifty foot diameter, hockey puck-shaped center, and sported another couple of occupied chairs.

"We're sorry," said Micmac. "Didn't see it coming at all."

Crayle responded. "Ditto for us."

All four captives turned to a commotion emanating from the third tunnel, a third spoke in the subterranean wheel.

"*Whine!*" came the outcry.

"STFU, Lenny!" Alona admonished. "We're in serious trouble."

The chairs that contained the Lipschitz couple arrived fastened to the back of a highly modified electric Smart car. The roof had been structurally strengthened to protect its occupants from falling rocks. At the third tunnel's end, the autonomous vehicle turned and deposited the chairs.

The final two seats had been placed. With Lenny now quiescent, the six members of the Crayle spy team just stared at each other. No words were spoken.

CHAPTER 50

As three bicycle wheel spokes converged at a wheel's hub, the three mining tunnels converged underground near the famous Ulurú rock. There, the six Crayle team members awoke, still strapped securely to the minimalist chairs.

They'd been arranged in pairs and found themselves sitting two-by-two, each pair situated so as to be centered in their own tunnel end. They faced inward to the circular convergence of the tunnels. The particular arrangement allowed each sub-grouping of team members to face the other two.

Australian Hamilton Farrell and his adjutant, Kianna Tarni, stood in the round central area outside the lowered Cultural Centre regarding their captives. The Aussie spoke.

"Now that I've dispensed with the formality of greeting you as separate couples, I'd like to welcome you to the Red Centre's most illustrious site, Ulurú. It, of course, cannot be viewed from our subterranean location, but I imagine that is, at the moment, of little concern to any of you. You wish to go back to the U.S.A. and live quiet family lives away from people like me. I'm afraid that your lack of cooperation up to this point makes that outcome … unlikely. So, that said, there are some people I would like you to meet."

The Australian and Kianna stepped around and assumed positions behind Lenny and Alona. The darkness cast by the tunnel behind them made them barely recognizable.

Footsteps echoed as individuals traversing the dark holes behind each of the remaining Crayle team pairs approached.

The two who positioned behind Phoebe and Micmac caused a jaw to drop. Lenny's. The astonished P.I. exclaimed, "Wait, wait, wait! They caught you, too?"

The blonde woman responded. "No, Mr. Lipschitz. They did not. Let me introduce you to my very talented, and beloved, sister, whom you did not chance to meet. This is Astrid as you would know her. The crypto-currency IT expert. Her real given name … Crystel. Although you have known me …" She glanced at Alona. "… in the non-biblical sense as Heidi, that name is likewise fake. I am Alice." She pronounced it in the French manner—*ah-leese*. "It means noble and graceful."

Lenny felt as if he'd been slapped several times.

Crayle had it. "This whole thing about our money was a sham, wasn't it? You're working for Farrell."

Hekka picked up their train of thought. "You used Lenny to lure us all to southeastern America, where this man's killers …" She nodded at Auger. "… could take us out." She tried to turn her head, but wooden paddles that restricted side vision and head movement affixed to each of the chairs precluded it.

"We are nearly finished here, Mr. and Mrs. Crayle."

The two heard steps. From behind them this time. The echo of footsteps in the tunnel.

As the newcomers pulled up behind the Crayles, both saw across the central hub four jaws drop. Four sets of eyes opened wide. Beyond disbelief.

A female placed her hands around Hekka's neck. She squeezed. Just enough that her victim gasped for breath.

"Oh, we mustn't do that," the woman whispered. She relaxed her grip and pulled her hands back to the shoulder tops. "Your baby will need air. At least, for now." Slowly, she pushed her hands down the front of Hekka's blouse. "Nice and full, but your baby won't need them."

Hekka struggled against her bonds.

Crayle, who'd heard every word, likewise.

The spy-quality Velcro thwarted their every effort to break free.

The man, obviously aroused by his partner's actions, stepped around Crayle.

Crayle ended his struggle with the bonds.

"Lalumière!"

In that instant, he knew who molested his wife.

She stepped into view.

"Pattie! No! No! You're dead! We saw you from the submarine off Monte Carlo! Thrown by the mini-nuke explosion into the Mediterranean! Dead!"

"Omigod!" Hekka cried out. "Omigod!"

She struggled with all her might to break free.

Too much.

Her head dropped to her chest.

Fainted.

Lalumière remained unphased by what had just transpired. He provided the requisite journal of the recent past.

"I was sequestered just like the original Man In The Iron Mask on Sainte Marguerite Island, just one-half mile off Cannes, when the Monte Carlo bomb exploded. Heart stricken by a mushroom cloud to the east that surely portended the death of my exceptional wife. And I, formally declared the new King of France by the Prince of Monaco and the pope—both taken by the same explosion—was in that instant deprived of my queen. I was grief stricken. I would have to rule alone. It was my saddest day."

"But I got away," Pattie continued as she stroked Hekka's shiny black tresses. "The force from my bomb blew from the Formula One victor's ceremony in front of the Hôtel de Paris in the elevated Casino Square, through the casino, through the Fairmont Hotel, and over the top onto the waterside road, sucking rather than pushing me into the Med. You do understand sucking, don't you, Magus?" She glanced over at her husband.

"No," Lalumière said. "You may not have him one last time."

Pattie returned her gaze to the man she so wanted to compromise.

"It seems I'm predictable."

Crayle seethed. "Like any psychopath."

"Oh, how sad. Parting will be such sweet sorrow."

The Aussie resumed control. "The schedule, I'm afraid, requires us to bid adieu at this point. I must confess that the six of you have been excellent adversaries to our Illuminé dreams. In a few minutes, your opposition will be just so much un-shared history. We shall all be safely back at the three respective mines and away by the time these bombs detonate. As I'm sure you've guessed, the force of those out of control atoms will concentrate in the central hub you face. At that time, the force will carry upward, dissolving the sacred Ulurú into a fine, red mist to be carried across the land. And with that event, the convergence of the aboriginals and their protectors, the rest of Australia, will overthrow the Canberra politicians, and I, Hamilton Farrell, shall seize power. Total power."

"And we, Pattie and I," Lalumière added, "will return to France. Our coronation is scheduled for next week. We'd invite you, but you won't be attending. Oh, I almost forgot to tell you. Alice and Crystel? They're my daughters."

"Eighty-seven hundred degrees Fahrenheit," Farrell interjected. "I really must apologize. There will be no funerals for you six. You can't bury vapor."

He gave the order to his Feral guard and to his guests, all of whom, having heard his words, achieved a severely anxious state.

All but the six Crayle team members started down the tunnels to their electric vehicles.

Crayle yelled after them, "Your times will come! You'll rot in Hell!"

"All of you!" Hekka cried out.

The Aussie stopped for a second. He spun on his heel.

"Then see that we receive a proper reception. When *our* time comes."

As the two turned to follow the rest, the Aussie had a last thought. "Kianna, my dear. Please stay behind and check their bindings one more time. We wouldn't want them to miss the finale." He laughed, but before he started back to the first of two Golf Cars, he admonished her. "Don't dally. There are just fifteen minutes on the clock for us to get back and away. I've grown quite fond of you."

"I'm just about free," Micmac whispered.

Unfortunately, the walls, floors, and ceilings of their respective tunnels were of solid rock. His words caught the Australian in mid-stride. The Aussie stopped. He turned to his assistant.

"As I said. Ensure that the bonds are still fast. We wouldn't want them to run in vain for their lives." He laughed. "And give them each a little kiss. Goodbye."

CHAPTER 51

Kianna watched him depart, then made the circular tour of the captives, checking their tethers. She stopped behind the last, then bent over to whisper softly into Hekka's ear. She leaned down to place a long dark object in her hands. Last, she planted a final whisper in Phoebe's ear.

"I believe this is goodbye. Good luck." She hopped aboard the last vehicle and chased after the Aussie.

"Good luck?" said Lenny. "Three atomic bombs a few feet away and … good luck?"

The bomb timers ticked louder and louder as they counted down. Their ominous sound reverberated an ever certain finality off the tunnels' red walls.

The breathing among the three couples grew heavy and increased apace. The individual tension escalated as if to best a previous upper threshold.

Finally, "*No!*" Alona cried.

"What happened?" Lenny yelled.

"My … my water broke!"

Then, "*Oh!*"

Phoebe.

"*Oh!*"

Hekka.

Three women. Three waters.

The men went shell-shocked as they stared at the puddles. Transfixed.

Reality yanked them back.

"Fifteen minutes," Crayle cried out.

Before he could utter another word, Hekka snapped both hands in front. One bore the Bowie knife just placed in her grasp. "I don't know why she did it, but we owe something to that Kianna. And her people."

As quickly as possible, she freed the others and ignored Lenny when he asked, "Where'd you get that?"

Crayle glanced up at the ceiling. "Bomb timers reaching a crescendo. Three mini-nukes prepared to go postal. And three pregnant women going into labor," the aspiring thriller novelist muttered. "You can't make this up."

He returned quickly to the present situation.

"We can't escape three directional mini-nukes pointed to collide and multiply their forces at the center."

He checked faces for any semblance of an idea.

He called to Micmac. "There's no way we can distance ourselves far enough! See if there's a way to shut them down!"

"Not without a special key."

"Not good."

Micmac yelled back. "Wait! Everybody! I saw something as the thugs brought us in!"

"Make it fast!" Crayle replied.

"A sign on the bomb in my tunnel! FRONT TOWARD ENEMY! They're directional! Like Claymores!"

"That's it!" Phoebe cried. "The aboriginal woman whispered in my ear, D-F-N-D."

"Of course." Micmac, the weapons specialist, knew. "Directional Force Nuclear Device."

"I can pronounce that acronym," Lenny offered. "Deafened."

"Defend," Micmac corrected.

In that instant, Crayle knew what they must do.

"Everybody! Run! Toward the bombs!"

"Great idea!" Lenny yelled back.

"No! I've got it!" Crayle cried out. "Grab the carriage handles, and spin them around 180 degrees. Pointing outward from the center. Meet back here! At the hub!"

The men did their best as they tried to assist each of their wives.

Very determined, Hekka, Phoebe, and Alona loped to the bomb carts to help.

They did as Crayle instructed.

In his tunnel with Hekka, Crayle could not see the other two couples. He used the tunnels' natural reverberance to amplify his voice. "Back to the Cultural Centre in the middle! Our elevator! Out of here!"

Having rotated the bombs, the six moved as fast as collectively possible back to the hub and entered the still-lowered Cultural Centre.

The women did their best, squeezing out the last remnants of fluids as they jogged alongside their men.

"We're down to about ten minutes!" Crayle yelled.

As they entered the central hub, he shoved them ahead to ensure that all would make it.

Finished underground, they scampered into the Cultural Centre entrance, and former Navy sailor Micmac called out, "Prepare to surface. One floor up, please."

Crayle punched the starred **1** button.

The facility didn't move.

The bomb timers' portent of doom not far away increased to deafening.

He punched the button again and again.

Finally, a computer-synthesized voice startled them. "Door closing."

The least of their worries.

The huge elevator jerked, and started upward.

The multi-purpose Ulurú Cultural Centre rose at a snail's pace. With forty vertical feet to transit, the building arrived topside in seconds that seemed like hours.

Above ground, they ran out through the doors.

An out of breath Crayle gasped, "Pointless to run. Ladies, find a spot. Be seated. Please."

They did, but their respite was brief.

Heartbeats echoed off the walls.

CHAPTER 52

Normally, three standard mini-nuke bombs would explode each of their areas upward and outward to form three rising mushroom clouds. Normally.

When the clock struck zero, the bombs detonated in unison.

One huge **Boom!** from below.

The entire force of each device blew air, rock, and anything else in their path down its tunnel corridor at warp speed.

By their nature, they caused very little effect in the tunnels' hub. Because the devices had been reversed, the full force of each bomb travelled away, toward the three mines. The destruction simultaneously struck the equidistant diamond, gold, and uranium mines.

Each being at the terminus of a tunnel, the force erupted skyward as if the bombs had been situated immediately beneath the surface. The eruptions through the solid rock gave the entire area, and the Centre containing the Crayle clan, a violent shake.

The fire and fury incinerated the contents of each mine—equipment, on-duty crews, and Feral guardsmen—in that instant. When the outcome of the intense tumult completed, the bulk of the mines would be buried for eternity.

The Crayles, the MacKays, and the Lipschitzes witnessed the enormous expulsion of rock, dust, and air at each of the tunnel ends almost two miles away.

The ground buckled and shook.

"Inside! Quick!" Crayle yelled.

No sooner than they dashed back inside, airborne debris from the periphery of the three-spoke wheel of tunnels rained down like lead-filled snowflakes.

Lenny hollered, "Fetal position!"

"You get fetalized like me and try to scrunch up!" Alona retorted.

Crayle interceded. "Everyone! Sit on the floor! Cover your heads!"

The rainfall of rubble continued for the next twenty minutes non-stop. From time to time, a fractional boulder penetrated their shelter.

None of them moved. They didn't know where the next inert missile might land.

When the furor subsided to zero, they peeked outside.

All safe.

In the distance they viewed in awe three perfectly formed mushroom clouds. When the clouds began to disfigure and blow away, they looked back down to their immediate periphery.

Littered about the outside of the Cultural Centre lay hundred of glittering chunks of gold-bearing ore, a smattering of yellow cake uranium, and hundreds upon hundreds of raw diamonds.

"We're back to diamonds, gang," Crayle announced.

A light rain began to fall.

Although the diamonds were raw and uncut, the visual energy and beauty inside could not be contained.

Crayle observed the sparkle before them. It brought a big, overdue smile.

"Water Diamonds."

Their troubles, abated for the moment, weren't quite finished.

"Oh, crap!" cried Phoebe.

"Me, too!" followed Alona.

"Make that three!" Hekka exclaimed. "Due dates … *now!*"

"Guys!" Crayle, driven nearly breathless by the past five seconds, pointed at a wall. "Grab those Abo blankets!"

• • •

Men delivering babies proved not to be a new or original concept. Three pregnant women. Three dilapidated men. Three babies.

CHAPTER 53

After three weeks of seclusion and the departure of Micmac, Phoebe, Lenny, Alona, and their new babies back to the U.S., the Australian military transported Magus, Hekka, and Baby Crayle out of the Red Centre. They were deposited at the Australian northeast coastal city, Port Douglas. Preprinted tickets in hand, they readied themselves mentally for some serious rest and relaxation. R & R.

A catamaran tour boat labeled Wavedancer dropped off those, like the Crayles, who possessed tickets for the eponymously sized Low Isles. Most would snorkel the waters of the Great Barrier Reef. Except two.

"Oh, I forgot to tell you. Stones set us up for this trip."

"Stones, as in the American president. When did you talk to him?"

"At the military base. Anyway, here's what he said." Crayle puffed up his chest and provided his interpretation of the call. "Can't let you go anywhere. All the boards and computers around here have been lit up like a Chinese fireworks factory gone ballistic. I'm going to put you two … three … where you'll be out of danger."

"How considerate. Do you know anything about this place?"

"They read me in on the plane, Hekka. The uninhabited one of these two ocean specks is Woody Island. Ours, Low Island, is laid out like a bulls-eye. The center is jungle with nothing but a lighthouse. A wide ring of soft, warm sand separates that from the ocean. Part of the Great Barrier Reef is just offshore."

"They must've delivered that intel in the bathroom, because that's the only time you were out of my sight."

"They call it a head. It's quite secure."

That brought a smile.

"Follow me, Hekka," Crayle said once they alighted from the boat. "We'll circle the island by foot. It's not far."

As Hekka padded through the sand, a serious thought invaded her mind. "Is there a hospital on this little island?" She glanced down at the swaddled infant in her arms. "How did you know what to do?"

"Well, for their 200,000 years of existence, humans had babies without modern medicine."

"Don't give me that. How'd you know? The Farm?"

"Not me. I was sick the day they had the baby delivery lecture. I knew I forgot to tell you something." Crayle smiled. "I did watch a TV course once on delivery techniques. And I can boil water."

"Sea water?"

"I've got a little surprise."

"So have I. Let's stay awhile. I'm just not ready to expose her to the world quite yet."

"I believe the planet could use one more on the good side."

"It turns out we need more females. You know, to bring peace to the planet."

They rounded the circular island until the soft sand gave way to strata of volcanic rock. Flat on top, it appeared to be a landing area for people hopping off of boats.

"I'll give you this one, Magus. That is stunning. Let's just stand here and be amazed."

Twenty minutes later, Crayle led them into the jungle aspect of the island until they reached a wooden sign.

"A famous gravesite that way."

She started along a very narrow path.

"No, no. Check the ground there. See those holes. Snakes."

Hekka retraced. "We've battled enough of the human variety. I shall forego any further contact."

No more than fifty yards further, they came upon a white, two-story cottage with a work shed nearby.

"This is it. Our home for the night."

She pointed to a sign nearby. "It's the lighthouse keeper's residence. Did you set this up on one of those dot com sites?"

"It's abandoned. The lighthouse is no longer in use. But, I've been informed that there is water in the tower above, and food in the fridge. And the darkened windows should provide us the privacy we'll require to try for baby two."

"Looks like baby one and I need to climb stairs to the second story. At least there's a nice covered deck before you go inside. We can rest there."

"Check out the sign next to the stairs. 'No Sand … No Wetsuit' will not be a problem."

He clunked his shoes on the side of the stairway. Collected sand fell harmlessly.

Hekka followed suit and both headed up.

She glanced over at him with a slightly suspicious look. "You know. President's aren't the ones who do the details. Don't tell me that our Nova Scotia Darryl colleague set this up for us. If so, we're going to owe him a serious amount of his favorite Canadian beer."

• • •

Late the next morning, the two were still in bed. A late sleeping baby accounted for the gratuitous lethargy.

"What are you doing, Mr. Crayle?"

"Our daughter is going to need a little brother. Let's see if I remember how it's done."

"What, since last night?"

They fell asleep satisfied and fully relaxed, with the exception of the periodic feedings and other attentive measures required by their newborn, until two thirty in the morning.

Crayle sat up. "What was that?"

"Do they have earthquakes here?"

"I'm afraid they do. Quick, get under the bed!"

"Sure. I can do that with my new tummy."

"Oh, crap!"

"If I was full of it, then crapping might help. Are you saying ..."

"You're not working with me here. You're channeling Lenny's sense of humor."

"Whine."

He jumped up and ran to the window, yanking apart the curtains.

What they saw caused them both to catch their breaths.

The same sort of rock surface they'd seen at the beach passed view from window bottom to window top.

"We're sinking. But not by nature's call."

The motion stopped with a jarring thud.

Crayle returned to the bed and took a seat at Hekka's side.

"Not good."

"What's not good?"

"Remember Neil Wohlford? The Illuminé implant at the CIA? Jack Sommer's boss?"

"Sure. He's dead. Pattie did him over in his homeland. France."

"He's the one who spec'd the Quarry Hospital just north of Big Bear. And the covert cathedral in Washington, D.C. And Jack's office in Manassas. Notice any similarities?"

"Oh, brother, do I. All three are about 300 feet underground. Do you think ..."

"I recall one of our teammates thinking that Wohlford was being clever. The underground sites would, to the very insightful, indicate a mole."

"But mole Wohlford is very, very dead. Certified, in fact."

"I'm afraid the secret society, Illuminé, is not. I'll check the attic for any way out of here. Cross your fingers." He glanced at their sleeping child. "You, too." He left.

The vigorous motions of the Crayles lying on the bed caused a stir nearby. The crying baby wakened the new parents.

Crayle scanned the room.

Hekka grabbed the baby, then turned to him. "None of that happened."

"My God." He stared straight into her eyes. "We had the very same dream. At the same time. I need to set up an appointment with Doctor Rorschach."

• • •

The next morning, Hekka found a message from her husband. "Found snorkeling gear in closet. Going to test nature. Be back by lunch. Love you."

He'd taken a mask, snorkel, and pair of fins from a closet. He walked through the jungle-like flora to the beach, donned the gear, and snorkeled offshore with a nurse shark nearby.

With encrypted comms fully restored to all team members, Micmac had already provided intel by means of a secure text message regarding sea life on The Barrier Reef, so Crayle knew that this particular species wouldn't harm him. He viewed it as an incarnation of Hekka looking after him.

Without warning, a scuba diver arrived on the scene via sea scooter with deadly weapons. He wore a diver's dry suit with a bubble top reminiscent of an upside down test tube.

Crayle recognized the Aussie BG, now devoid of empire and plans, trying to kill the man who brought him down.

His enemy's craft sported several gas-powered spear guns arrayed on either side. All he could bring to the battle was Hekka's Bowie strapped to his thigh. Bringing a knife to a speargun fight flashed through his mind. Still, it was his only possible defense. He couldn't outswim the sea scooter. Or its spears.

But it seemed that the mining mogul was not adept with his weapons. He fired and fired, but Crayle deflected each shot with Hekka's knife.

The Aussie stopped. Out of ammunition.

And not in possession of the scuba tank setup of his attacker, Crayle would soon be out of air.

The magnitude of his quandary was obvious.

A trip to the surface would deprive him of the visual. The one he needed to deflect any further attacks.

If he didn't, he'd drown.

That was not the end to Crayle's lethal encounter.

At that very moment, a bull shark, believed to be the most dangerous shark species in the world, arrived on the scene.

As Crayle turned back to face the first menace, he was shocked. The man had left the sea craft and was now right in front of him.

They battled.

The Aussie was much better with his knife than he'd been with the spear guns. He wounded Crayle.

Then, he backed off.

Why?

The blood in the water attracted the bull. He closed in at kill speed.

Crayle refused to die. A vision of Hekka and their new baby flashed across his mind.

The bull shark closed at full speed.

At the last second, the nurse shark flew by and swam between them. She butted the bull on the nose.

Hamilton Farrell observed it all with a smile. He looked certain the bull would devour Crayle.

But the nurse proved too determined.

Rather than deal with an angry female, the bull shark darted for the Australian, and took a big bite.

The victim of his own clever scheme, Farrell's eyes popped wide.

His jaw fell, dropping the scuba mouthpiece to his chest.

Bubbles spewed from his mouth as he screamed with pain.

Crayle nodded to the nurse shark as the bull carried off its prey. He'd never think an evil thought about an RN again.

Back on land, he stopped the bleeding and traipsed back at the lightkeeper's house. He lumbered inside with both gear and himself dripping water and wet sand on the floor. Somehow, he conjured the appropriate words in response to *Hi, sweetheart. How'd it go?*

"Oh, not much going on. Nice at the Reef. Better here."

CHAPTER 54

Inside the lighthouse keeper's abode, an exhausted Magus Crayle stepped into the kitchen area to find Hekka, back to him, working over the counter. She seemed to struggle with a dull kitchen knife.

He loved the way she looked, took a moment to appreciate the sight, then set her Bowie on the counter.

She quickly swapped it for the more typical, though unsharpened, utensil.

"So, what's for dinner, darling?"

She smiled. She absolutely loved to prepare meals for him.

"Shark Fin Soup, dear."

"Sounds delicious."

He scanned the living room for a place to sit. The furnishings of the Lighthouse Keeper's dwelling on The Great Barrier Reef's Low Isles were distinctly period. Nineteenth Century, to be exact. Hmmm. Couch. Loveseat. Rocking chair. Arm chairs. He headed for the chair least likely to collapse from its age and his weight.

Unexpectedly, someone stepped out of the bedroom. Crayle's eyes searched for the first-available weapon.

From the kitchen, Hekka put that need to rest. "She's one of us, Magus."

His eyes focused anxiously on the person in the doorway. Life expectancy improved dramatically for a spy who took nothing at face value.

"One of us? She told you that? You believe her?"

"I do. And you know I wouldn't be taking any chances with you … or with our little one. She arrived just thirty minutes ago, and told me her story. You need to hear it.

Kianna Tarni, Hamilton Farrell's adjutant and soothsayer, stepped into the room. She removed a small purple, strap-hung purse from the shoulder of her small, color-matched dress, and handed it to Crayle. "My purple and black 9mm Beretta Nano is inside. Otherwise, I'm unarmed."

Crayle viewed the stunning aboriginal with suspicion. "Anytime a woman declares herself to be unarmed, I become even more worried. Hekka, please certify that her tiny, skin-tight dress holds no surprises."

Uncharacteristically, and as if she knew something material that Crayle did not, Hekka giggled.

"I mean …"

Kianna tossed a furtive glance at each of them. "I can take it off." She reached back for the zipper.

"That won't be necessary." Hekka checked the only available location. "As Phoebe would say, '*Thighs. Clear!*'"

She headed back to the kitchen, which had been remodeled to provide open physical and visual access to the living room, but retaining the original styling.

"I just about have lunch ready. Feel free to use the love seat. Talk only."

Seated, Kianna began her story.

"A couple of years ago, I was assigned to get close to one Hamilton Farrell."

Crayle's stomach entered the conversation. "Speaking of lunch."

"Oh, I forgot a detail. I'm a member of ASIS—the Australian Secret Intelligence Service."

"Do you have creds I can check out? An ID? I have experience detecting forgeries."

"You know I wouldn't carry them on assignment. If I did, they'd be in my panties."

"Cute. Continue."

"There were suspicions that Ham—my pet name for him—was involved in some exotic secret society. No idea which one. I was to find out. And determine what he and they were up to in Australia, as well as what threat they might pose."

"And since your country is a member of Five Eyes, you, or someone in your organization, would have shared that intel with America's CIA, and the other three."

"Of course. Five Eyes is the long standing agreement among the English-speaking allies."

Crayle nodded affirmation.

She continued. "Long story short—I've picked up some Americanisms—Ham was Illuminé."

"Stop right there." Crayle caught his breath. "I believe he said that when we were captured, but we've seen no corroboration. You're sure?"

"One hundred percent, Mr. Crayle."

"If we're on the same side in the same deadly business, call me Magus."

"Magus. I like that." Kianna switched her gaze to Hekka. "Is he trying to flirt?"

Hekka turned, her favorite cutting utensil in hand. Her Bowie. "No. He's not flirting."

Crayle rescued himself. "Magus is derived from the word, Magic."

Kianna nodded her comprehension. "As in … Magic Man?"

He caught another, bigger breath. "You knew. You knew all along."

"That's why I placed that small sword of hers into her hand at the tunnel's hub. So she could set you all free."

"The three nuclear devices pointed in our direction and going off wouldn't have been to our advantage, would they?"

"Our Code Name: Magic Man dossier. When I witnessed from far away those horrendous explosions at the three mines, I knew what you'd accomplished. But, there's more. As you learned, the portable carriages for the bombs possessed a wheel-locking mechanism that required a very special barrel key. Ham trusted me with it. I switched them off."

"So we could spin them around."

She nodded.

"Perhaps there's a Magic Woman in the room."

Hekka turned, holding the Bowie, point upward. "Now, he's flirting."

"A second Magic Woman. That's what I meant."

"Good save," Hekka said, returning to her lunch-making.

"Resourceful and quick." The lady in purple smiled.

Hekka responded. "Necessary traits of a spy."

"There's more," the aboriginal continued. "The Illuminé, as you are aware, have been utilizing miniaturized nuclear weapons to reshape the global political landscape."

"Yes, we know." Crayle chose not to own up to the deadly nuclear Blackstone Strategy he'd formulated a few years earlier.

"He was after Australia. He tried to remove New Zealand as a threat at that rugby match, where your associate ran off with the bomb. Ham referred to him as an irritating, diminutive pest."

"Lenny's heard that before. Trust me."

"Ham received that first bomb from his Chinese source. Proof of concept, he said. Earlier, he'd transported uranium from Mine #3 to Shanghai, hidden in one of his many coal shipments. He fetched the three mini-nukes, he called them, on the return trip."

"How'd he avoid detection of the radiation from the bombs at the ports?"

"The Chinese supplied him with special blankets made from materials called Radiation Sponges. Are you familiar?"

Crayle was quite familiar. It got worse. Ling would have to have known about this transaction, and, with little doubt, authorized it. Especially for him, a hard pill to swallow. "The Chinese cover their bombs with a honeycomb of the material. Lots of devastation, but later inhabitable devastation."

"You have something you need to say. I'm listening."

Crayle definitely had more to say. Now was as good a time as any.

"I went for a dive earlier. The man, Farrell, found me. Tried to kill me. But listen to me. I know that, when you've gone dark and cold and spent some time with a target, you can't help but acquire an attachment … and feelings. Kianna, Hamilton Farrell is dead."

She didn't react as he expected. "I know. I implanted a nano-cam on him. I witnessed it in real time."

A tear formed and slipped down her cheek. "It's too easy to judge him now. In being with him, I learned that his upbringing was strict and effective. His father and mother were quite religious. He was to be a man of virtue."

"What happened?"

"The switch from coal to gold, diamonds, and uranium caused him to change. The Illuminé recruited him. They know their business when it comes to acquiring someone they can transform. Then take all the righteousness and vigor and mold it to what they want. To what they need. I've seen something similar in my country when people first begin with drugs. In a fairly brief time, their whole attitude toward the subject changes. The entry level substances become mid-level. Then, serious. So many die here for that reason. Starting is the critical error."

"So he got into drugs?"

"No. My analogy transfers over, though. His drug was power. The mines brought him power at the first level. After that, it was about more power. The Illuminé promised him Australia. Then his mind took that as a second stepping stone to the top drug. That of the Elder he thought would someday rule the planet. Like the drug people, the power types become narcissists, unable to care about anyone other than themselves. Who they hurt in the process is immaterial. Only what they themselves obtain counts."

"I get what you're saying. He went from a man of virtue to one without. His whole life was a virtue transition." He turned to Hekka. "How about that? Hamilton Farrell did have a good idea. A future book title. The Virtue Transition."

He produced a 'what do you think' glance at Hekka. "Write it down, Ian."

"I'm not Ian Fleming. In order to be a successful novelist, I have to be unique."

"From what I've witnessed, author Crayle, you are nothing if not unique."

Hekka responded with, "Amen."

Crayle turned back to their guest.

"What now for you? It appears that this Illuminé Vice Elder and many of his Ferals are gone."

"As in America, Illuminé place their minions in key strategic and tactical civil positions, to cause the most sedition—undermining of the government. There will be more to root out. I have specific expertise and experiences now to define and commission operations."

"A promotion?"

"Yes."

Crayle tilted his head. "There's a bit more."

"Oh, how could I forget. Ham intended to take over our country by means of the destruction of the Ulurú, but it wasn't his end game. Wanna hear?"

"She's channeling Lenny," Hekka observed.

Kianna gave them a smile. "His goal, his dream, his fantasy was to replace the previous Illuminé Elder—the Prince of

Monaco—destroyed by the Monte Carlo bomb, as the society's Supreme Leader."

"Well, that's off the table."

"And Australia owes you a great deal, Magus. But there appears to be someone of interest in South America. Someone who took issue with Ham's greatest desire; someone who has, due to your self-defense move, just lost his primary opposition. Another Vice Elder. But that issue is for later."

From the kitchen, "There! Done!" Hekka ported two large bowls replete with large spoons, and set them before her lunch guests. She fetched a third and plopped into the rocking chair facing them.

The pair on the love seat leaned over the vessels and peered inside. Catching the aroma, they turned to each other with a puzzled look. Then, at Hekka.

"Shark Fin Soup. Dig in."

They did.

"Delicious," Hekka nodded. "And, Mr. Crayle, you're not the only problem-solver in the room."

"I'm not?"

"The back and forth over what to name our baby … is over."

Her impromptu insertion of their new child surprised him. He listened.

"In honor of the lady superhero seated across from you, the one who saved all of our lives, I give you …" She held up the baby. "Kianna."

CHAPTER 55

The late afternoon brought a cold, heavy rain to Hong Kong and its Imperial Palace, the latter perched high atop Victoria Peak.

Inside, Ling An-yee, new empress of all China, sat in her royal lounge chair. Next to her, a fish bowl situated atop the thousand-year-old side table left just enough space for her evening tea, which would soon arrive. Not just any bowl or fish, they represented a parting gift from the orphanage—upon her purchase by adoptive father, the deceased Emperor Chin Yao-wu.

She thought of the stock market mogul who'd taken her in, provided a superb education, and then made her his wife. His personal past, she realized, transformed a normal, full relationship with any woman into a monumental step for the late emperor. She knew she'd been that special to him.

And her. From orphan with little hope to empress of China. She'd been fifteen at the time of her adoption. Since Chin demanded the brightest of the lot, the orphanage fudged birth records so he would never look elsewhere. In five short, but quite active years, she'd lived nearly every minute with her eleven *siblings* in isolation and under the control of the man they knew as Father.

But that was just history. The intrigues going forward could surpass those of the past. Of necessity, she'd employed the remnants of the former government's Standing Committee, the highest political echelon. That Chin declared communism to no longer exist meant the committee personnel served only to operate the government, not to spread or maintain any ideological doctrine. To do so, they'd been informed, would invoke swift and excruciating capital punishment.

Additional threats to her reign existed. White Daughter carried the male child of Chin. And what about Yellow Daughter? She'd always been a trusted confidant, loyal and efficient to a fault.

At that mesmerized moment, Yellow brought in the evening tea as she'd done so many times before.

Ling offered a courteous smile as Yellow placed the full cup on the table, provided the requisite bow of obeisance, then left the room through a pair of tall drapes. No need to worry further. At least, not about Yellow. She was more than an able courtier. She was, by law of adoption and their years together, a sister.

Ling took the cup into her hands. As the essence of the hot liquid wafted toward the ceiling, Ling looked down into the cup's depths. Then, she gazed back to where Yellow had exited.

She wouldn't.

Of course not.

Acting on pure instinct, Ling poured the tea into the fish bowl and shifted her focus to the tall drapes. How stupid of her. She trusted Yellow most of all.

Her other trusted source always produced a calm that enabled wisdom.

She glanced back at the bowl.

Ling recoiled. She gasped.

Dead.

All of them.

Dead.

Severe anguish and fear caused her to grab her phone.

She tapped in the speed-dial code, then hit the ***Call*** icon.

As the dial tone pulsed, the name at the top of the screen seemed to throb.

The one she needed now.

Magus Crayle.

EPILOGUE

It seemed that, whenever there appeared to be a cessation of hostile acts by global entities, it was not to be taken as an ascendance toward peace. Rather, it was a time to plot and re-plot, always seeking an end game where most of the world's population would suffer. The old American motto that preached Life, Liberty, and the Pursuit of Happiness struggled to escape the boundaries of that country, and, in some instances, seemed to struggle within them. For their part, the Crayle team continued to rack up points, saving both people and places, and the ever victimized lot known in the political, military, and espionage trades as collateral. The team, now well funded outside the auspices and control of the government, would continue its quest. It would play the hand it was dealt at any point in time, do its best with that, and endeavor always to draw a better hand. The following sitrep is as they are all. A report of the situation as of the moment. And the moment, as it always did, would change … momentarily.

THE CHINESE

Empress Ling didn't choose to watch media reports on the television. Rather, she relied on a designated courtier to peruse the material, then provide her a daily briefing much like that received by American presidents.

"There were three atomic detonations in Australia's Red Centre. Some peripheral damage. Total destruction of our client's three mines."

"Very strange. Why would he do that?"

"I don't know, but he's missing."

"Bad for business."

THE GERMANS

The lady chancellor had become worried about an Aryan resurgence. They still existed, her advisors had informed her, but had waxed quiescent. Where?

THE FRENCH PEOPLE

After a long drought, the French people began to receive new pronouncements from the famous Mitim. Morose since his disappearance, their elation returned. And hope. A nationwide survey by Le Monde indicated a 98% approval rating.

THE SWEDES

The situation in Sweden was currently up in the air. Russia remained a threat as long as Vladimir held the reins. The czarina gained popularity with the people of the country apace. The queen wondered who would reach the finish line first. The czarina in Russia, or herself, the Queen of Sweden.

THE VATICAN

The new pope was fully engaged, preparing for his duties in Paris in the forthcoming weeks. That the French, especially without their leaders, would actually make a scheduled deadline exceeded iffy. But, he'd already received verification of eligibility and marital rites performed. So, he'd be there regardless. It was just for the mysterious and seldom seen pair that he'd publicly crown king and queen to show up.

THE AMERICANS

When the information had been leaked to the world press that one Lenny Lipschitz had spotted the mini-nuke at New Zealand's Eden Park stadium, and had saved both Kiwi and Aussie rugby teams, as well as an arena full of fans and much of Auckland, he was named a national hero … in both countries. Through CIA back channels, Jack Sommers determined that Kianna Tarni had magically recovered the actual historical ball from Farrell's stack of collectibles, and saw that it was returned it to its rightful place in Lenny's name.

Back in America and upon notification of the awards, the P.I. became quite difficult to be around.

Lenny, by the way, had stuffed the nuclear ball he'd fetched from the field into his backpack, which he subsequently stuffed into a closet at home. No one knew.

THE CRAYLES

Magus Crayle seriously considered taking the current opportunity to set spying aside, perhaps get his PhD in Mathematics. He'd discovered from his Rorschach memory restorations that he'd taken and passed all the classes, but he hadn't completed the comprehensive exams or a dissertation. A little CIA operation in China got in the way. He ran the notion by Hekka.

"I don't at all like to leave things undone. What do you think?"

She pondered a moment as she rocked their new baby.

"Well, there's one thing for sure. You'll be able to …"

"… do the math."

That cracked them up.

Even the baby laughed.

Crayle kept the feel good going. "Our girl officially graduated from Baby Crayle. We selected a name that, according to my intel, denotes consonance—harmony or agreement among components. It's perfect.

"Kianna Crayle," they chimed.

THE CRAYLES – GOLDENEYE

When the baby was old enough for travel, the Crayles found themselves at Jamaica's famous Goldeneye. Home away from home for spy novelist, Ian Fleming. With his first book out, and required reading at both Quantico and The Farm, Magus Crayle began to work on a second book. Perhaps of a crazed Chinese genius causing the world problems from a Caribbean island. There was a story there. Oh, but for a reader-grabbing title. He had it. Dr. No.

Crayle laughed at his silliness.

No one would put out real money for such an enigmatic, even silly, title.

Back to the drawing board.

THE FRENCHMAN

Sylvain Lalumière could not be found. Neither he nor his wife, associate, confidant received any part of the worldwide coverage of three miniature nuclear detonations in central Australia. Crayle noted that, since Farrell and Kianna definitely made it out of the mines in one piece, then his most severe of all enemies might have, as well. He also noted that the Frenchman had said something of serious import. The two of them were scheduled to attend a major event the next week. A coronation.

THE END

ABOUT THE AUTHOR

Committed to international affairs, political intrigue and espionage novelist Dennis Bowen has researched his stories in more than 60 countries. That Bowen engenders realism and spice in his thrillers due to his wartime service, and his defense and intelligence community background, led one reader to remark, "Bowen knows his stuff." *The Virtue Transition* follows *The Water Diamonds*, *The Blackstone Perfection*, *The Crystal Seduction*, *The Redrock Quarantine,* and *The Final Masquerade* as Book 6 in his International Thriller Series. When not traveling the globe to research his next thriller, he resides on the Southern California coast.

Facebook: http://www.facebook.com/DennisBowenThrillers/
Twitter: http://www.twitter.com/DBowenThrillers/
Website: http://www.dennisbowen.com/

THE
JASMINE NEGATIVE

BOOK 7:
INTERNATIONAL THRILLER SERIES

Available: Fall 2019

CHAPTER 1

The first bomb struck at 7:30 A.M. Getting to work in metro Los Angeles during morning rush hour repeated each day, each week, and so on with very little diversion from the norm. Thousands of cars, trucks, buses, and motorcycles performed daily like multitudinous streams of ants, each following the one in front. Those who didn't survive the commute found themselves carted off to the side like battlefield casualties.

Those who'd smuggled the first bomb into the Queen Mary, now a hotel in Long Beach, had smuggled a quite similar device onto the Queen Mary 2 just months earlier. With exceptional skill sets and otherworldly good fortune, the Crayle team thwarted the attempt by the Elder's Illuminé secret society to blow up New York.

Choosing the archived, original Queen seemed symbolic.

Like a giant carpet stretched north, south, and east, the land on which L.A. resided undulated as the Mary exploded into shards of molten hull iron, anchors, glass, and turned to vapor those who enjoyed what they believed to be a quiet hotel night aboard her away from home.

In the first instant, the brute force of the nuclear explosion struck the 405 Freeway segments and twenty-six miles west to Catalina Island. The freeways, much of them suspended in and wrapped around like steel reinforced pretzels, splintered in places, causing them to whip through the air like snakes.

Vehicles by the thousands were flung in all directions, many into the skyscrapers of the multitude of cities comprising metropolitan L.A.

Blowing away from shore, the blast caught three cruise ships headed out to sea. It crammed their noses into the roil of the Pacific and yanked free their rudders and screws. The latter, spinning at an insane rate of speed, blew west of the epicenter, cutting a swath through railroads, motor boats, and all else before bouncing up and cutting grooves through rich and poor residential districts alike.

L.A. was flattened like a steamroller crushing a vast extent of Tinker Toys and Lego's. The hurricane force winds slammed into the Santa Monica mountains, turning the famed HOLLYWOOD sign to creamy dust.

On the east side of the city, in the enclosed spaces of Disneyland's Pirates of the Caribbean, a vehicle had just commenced its slide at a very steep angle in the dark, heading for the much anticipated wet plunge at the bottom. Just as the riders readied for the impact, the second nuclear bomb struck. The cataclysmic force redefined the excitement typically rendered by the venerable E-Ticket.

At five megatons, all of the Disney property, all of surrounding Anaheim, and all other boroughs turned to molten goo.

Instead of cancelling each other as the bombs blasts clashed, they seemed to gather steam as the multiplied force moved east.

Fall 2019

THE JASMINE NEGATIVE

From
International Thriller Writer
DENNIS BOWEN

www.ingramcontent.com/pod-product-compliance
Lightning Source LLC
Chambersburg PA
CBHW020610310726
48979CB00008B/1414/J
* 9 7 8 1 7 3 2 5 6 1 0 0 7 *